RICHARD TYRRELL was born in Ireland and grew up in Dublin's Liberties district, the historic core of the city, and walked to school every day under the towering vats of the Guinness Brewery. He graduated in Pharmacology at University College Dublin but then took up writing. His poems have been published widely in literary magazines, and he was a trustee of the UK Poetry Society, serving as its first Irish Chairman.

He was a finalist in the Bruntwood Prize for Playwriting and on Channel 4's *The Play's the Thing*. He has been a late night DJ, worked at Wendys in Pittsburgh, copy-edited for an art historian, interviewed for *The Straits Times* of Singapore, written for the *Evening Standard*, *The Guardian*, *The Independent*, *The Sunday Times*, *The Times*, and reviewed for the *TLS* and *Literary Review*.

He is strongly influenced by Irish storytelling, especially Eddie Lenihan and his oral stories. He lives in Kensal Green, North West London, which is famous for its old cemetery, where the fox of the novel was first seen by Wilf.

THE FOX OF KENSAL GREEN

THE FOX OF KENSAL GREEN

RICHARD TYRRELL

CROMER

PUBLISHED BY SALT PUBLISHING 2026

2 4 6 8 10 9 7 5 3 1

Copyright © Richard Tyrrell 2026

Richard Tyrrell has asserted his right under the Copyright, Designs and Patents Act 1988 to be identified as the author of this work.

This book is sold subject to the condition that it shall not, by way of trade or otherwise, be lent, resold, hired out, or otherwise circulated without the publisher's prior consent in any form of binding or cover other than that in which it is published and without a similar condition including this condition being imposed on the subsequent publisher.

This book is a work of fiction. Any references to historical events, real people or real places are used fictitiously. Other names, characters, places and events are products of the author's imagination, and any resemblance to actual events or places or persons, living or dead, is entirely coincidental.

First published in Great Britain in 2026 by
Salt Publishing Ltd
12 Norwich Road, Cromer, Norfolk NR27 0AX, United Kingdom

GPSR representative
Matt Parsons matt.parsons@upi2mbooks.hr
UPI-2M PLUS d.o.o., Medulićeva 20, 10000 Zagreb, Croatia

www.saltpublishing.com

Salt Publishing Limited Reg. No. 5293401

A CIP catalogue record for this book is available from the British Library

ISBN 978 1 78463 366 0 (Paperback edition)
ISBN 978 1 78463 367 7 (Electronic edition)

Typeset in Neacademia by Salt Publishing

Printed and bound in Great Britain by Clays Ltd, Elcograf S.p.A.

i.m.
May Farrell
who loved foxes and all other animals, even crows

THE FOX OF KENSAL GREEN

PART 1
A MINORITY OF ONE

1

WILF Kelly was rich in time.

After the sudden death of his young mum thirty years ago, he lost his job. He'd swept bottles of wine onto the supermarket floor and stood in its mess, silent and swaying. The store fired him. He never found work again – and never tried. Time became his personal wealth.

Now he lived alone and clung to comforting routines, like his *Metro* round. Nobody bothered him except kids on the streets calling him 'Worzel', 'Beetlejuice' or 'Smelly Kelly'.

Sometimes they held up phones and filmed him. When he saw their malignant little hands rising, he put his head down and walked away.

He had lots of imaginary tormentors who were neighbours going about their business. Daily they looked at him with an expression of pity, tried to speak to him, and said things like, 'Are you okay, Wilf?'

2

ONE of his routines was to take walks in Kensal Green Cemetery. He loved its memorials, trees and bushes. His mum had told him thirty-three species of birds nested there. He picked blackberries each August, from a mass of brambles overgrowing a plot of 1910s graves. It was like the unbeating heart of London, where he could be ignored in peace.

On one of his regular strolls, his eye was caught by a flash of red among gravestones. The biggest fox he ever saw broke cover. It trotted onto the path and stopped to stare at him.

He saw its resentful eyes and the pale fur under its snout radiating into a chest ruffle. As abruptly as it stopped, it lost interest and twirled away into a thicket.

Wilf felt mesmerised and had to follow.

He crossed a rough patch, skirting graves verge by verge. He imagined his foot being sucked underground. Finally, he steadied himself on a Celtic cross and peered into the trees, trying to penetrate the foliage.

It was a big dog fox. Like him, it must live alone. It must go out at night foraging in the streets for fallen kebabs or fried chicken.

Wilf entered the thicket, ducking under branches. He saw another flash of red and made his keynote sound – one he often made when he saw people he knew or realised he was being stared at.

'Hrymmphh.'

The fox's head appeared from behind leaves. Its ears pointed forward as if Wilf had guessed its name in vulpine language. He said again,

'Hrymmphh.'

But that was the end. The animal fled. Wilf heard the swish of leaves as it loped away.

But he knew then and there his friend Felicia was right. If he was ever to be normal, he needed a pet.

3

FELICIA O'Dwyer was the only friend left in the tree streets neighbourhood who'd been in school with him. She was the same age and still lived on Yew Road in the house opposite his. She had children and grandchildren now.

When she was a crazy kid, her gang found an old bin and she curled up inside it while they rolled it on the Green. Felicia was spun and spun, laughing. Wilf watched from nearby. On an impulse, he jumped onto the bin and tried to run with its roll. He bobbled along for a few moments, then ended up flat on his face.

Felicia found it hilarious. But when her friends started to jeer him, she helped him up, licked her fingers and wiped grass from his cheeks.

'Piss off,' she told her mates.

From then on, he was in her protective custody. If someone nudged his arm as he drank milk at school, she threw milk at them. If someone barged into him, she barged into them. When a group of boys stood in a crescent crowding him, she kicked the biggest on the ankle.

'You know,' said her mother, who wasn't entirely comfortable with this, 'that little boy's not normal like you, Felly.'

'He's not stupid, Mam,' said Felicia. 'He's really clever.'

'All the same . . . don't get too involved.'

But Felicia ignored her mother's warning.

Most of the time, in school classes, he sat in a back corner, his eyes elsewhere. When they fell on her, she could sense him feel relief. She started sitting at the desk beside him. Occasionally, he whispered something to her, and she'd raise her hand and say, 'Sir, Wilf says the answer is . . .' He was always right.

After his mum's funeral, Felicia led him home and cooked a meal. And put plates of food in front of him, at least once a week, ever since. And did his laundry, coaxed him into her house for a hot shower, trimmed his hair and bought some, not all, of his clothes from charity shops.

He never said 'Hrymmphh' to her.

4

A few days before he saw the fox, he had been going through one of his morning routines. He ate his usual bowl of cornflakes, then took the box out to the street to give pigeons some breakfast too. He got a shock.

A car was in his space. Wilf didn't own a car but had a street parking space, where he left the recycling bins supplied by the Council. It used to be his mum's spot. The bins were pulled onto the pavement and a Skoda now stood like a squat coffin.

Normally, when his routines were disrupted, he swayed silently with his mind frozen. But now, he had an impulse to toss the pigeons' food onto the car.

He swooshed his arm with the toasted confetti, enjoying the sound as flakes rained on the metal. His donation was more generous than normal. But he left the surplus and stood back.

Pigeons came. Skittering and slipping on the shiny roof, scrabbling, pecking and soiling to their heart's content.

Wilf now wondered if he could lure a crow.

Felicia noticed all this from across the street. She often looked through her window around this time, to check what he was wearing or whether he was talking aloud.

She gave him a little time for himself before she ambled out. She had put on weight in recent years, and had fibroids, walking was sorer. Her neck felt huge and when she looked in mirrors she saw wobbling chins. But she knew that when Wilf saw her face, it was one he trusted.

'Wilf,' she said. 'You'll get into trouble. That makes people angry.'
'It's *my* space.'
'It isn't, it's the Council's and parking's hard to find.'
'They need a permit.'
'It might be in the post.'
'Is it?'
'It's where Council mail lives, love. Wilf, I've been thinking. Maybe it's time to get you a real pet. I mean, *pigeons*? They fly away.'
'A rat,' said Wilf, spitefully.
'I was thinking of a puppy.'
'A rat's the same size.'

'Okay. Let's leave it in the air for now. Think it over.'

'Good day to you, Felicia,' said Wilf.

Felicia thought that was the end. But he swung back again at his gate as something else crossed his mind.

'Look at the number plates. They're not British, they're Czech.'

'Did you expect a letter from the Czech Embassy?'

'No.'

'The car is Ana's parents'. They drove from Prague 'cos she's engaged and having a party. You'll hear serious noise Saturday – *I'm* invited. And another thing. This is an aspect of you I don't like, Wilf Kelly.'

Wilf stood his ground, but then looked at the ground, thought deeply, and went indoors.

5

FELICIA said he needed a pet. And now he'd gone to the cemetery and found one that felt right for him. He understood what she was thinking. Pets normalise outsiders. They somehow transform people in the eyes of others.

While he was sleeping, he had an odd dream. In it, he visited his mum's grave for the first time since her burial. He always avoided that patch on his walks. In his dream, two saplings planted by the sides of her grave grew into mature willow trees. Their crowns tilted to each other, as if shielding her from stormy skies.

In the ground, just where her womb would be, was a deep hole. From it, the fox squeezed out. It ignored him and refused to be scared away. It sat, hoisted a hind leg and began scratching behind its ear, like a house dog. It scratched so hard that the ground shook and the willows shed slender leaves and yellow catkins.

The dream woke him up next morning with a sense of what he understood to be love. 'To get love, you give love,' his mum used to chant when he was small, spreading her hand towards him and swinging it back towards herself. 'To get love, you give love,' she sing-songed.

Love meant gifts. He learned that if he helped her to dry the dishes, she gave him a gift, often a Flake bar, his favourite, or a pear.

Wilf decided to get a gift for his new pet.

6

So later that morning, after his *Metro* round, he invented a new routine. He chose a supermarket bag from the vast stock of bags, boxes and newspapers that cluttered up his house.

He walked up the Harrow Road to Jim Lyon's butcher shop.

It was a narrow shop, between a shisha café and a tyre store where a display tyre stood outside chained to a breeze block, to prevent it being stolen. Lyon's had a red sign saying, 'Freezer Meats', and in italics below, '*Wholesale prices*'.

His mum used to help Jim with accounts and paperwork when the shop first opened years ago. Jim had often visited their home. He'd sat the child on his knee and said, 'Look at my finger, Wilf, where is it?'

'Gone.'

'Too right, mate. That's what you get if you don't chop meat right.'

It was Friday morning and a long line of people stood outside Lyon's. Some bought orders of meat so heavy they had to walk to and from their cars, to put it into the trunks in relay.

Wilf joined the line, which fell muted. He noticed that newcomers left a berth behind him.

After ten minutes, he got inside the packed shop. Four butchers were plucking fare from glass units, whacking at racks of ribs with cleavers, pulling chickens from hooks, bagging and weighing, writing prices and adding them up by pencil. According to Jim, pencils kept minds agile. It was one of his mum's sayings too.

One butcher was young with his pencil behind his ear. He kept glancing at Wilf while filling an order. As soon as he finished, he ignored the people in front and came straight at him.

'What do you want?'

'Dog food.'

'Five kilos a tenner. How much do you want?'

Wilf, who had no money, said, 'I want to see Jim.'

'Why?'

'I want to see Jim,' said Wilf, loudly.

The store grew quiet, and the other butchers slowed down.

'He's out back,' said the man, scowling and peeling off the shop floor to the rear.

After a few moments, the ageing but still active figure of Jim emerged, wiping his nine fingers on a cloth.

'Wilf?' he said, surprised. 'How are you, mate?'

'Hrymmphh.'

'I haven't seen you since . . . don't know.' He paused. 'Are you okay? Were you locked away again?'

'No, they stopped the power and gas.'

'Who did?'

'Private companies.'

'How do you cook?'

'They stopped the power and gas.'

'You mean they left you with no heat or light?'

'Hrymmphh.'

'Do you need help?'

'No.'

'I see,' said Jim thoughtfully. 'Carbon zero and coping, mate. Fair dues to you. If I can't interest you in a side of pork, what'll I do you for?'

'Dog food.'

'Have you a dog now?'

'No.'

'You're not thinking of, like . . . eating it yourself?'

'I don't eat raw meat,' said Wilf loudly. 'Or runny eggs.'

A few of the customers started laughing. One of the Caribbean women said, 'Come to mine for jerk, love. You'd look good cleaned up.'

'Okay,' said Jim, generally. 'We're a little crowded. We get buyers in from the cafés and takeaways today. They keep us on our toes, you know. If you come back at closing time, we'll see you right.'

'Thanks,' said Wilf. But he stood there.

'I brought a bag,' he said, holding it up.

'Ah, I see,' said Jim. 'Well, give it here. We'll see you later, mate.'

Wilf nodded. He nodded at some of the other people as well, including the Caribbean lady.

'Hrymmphh,' he said mildly.

7

He waited anxiously all day and even neglected some routines. He didn't go to St. Aubert Church as he always did on Friday, for the free hot food the Vicar gave out.

'No one should ever go hungry,' said the Vicar each week as he distributed charity to a small flock of beggars and homeless.

In the evening, he returned to Lyon's and strode in behind the last shoppers. Pencil Ear reached under a chopping slab and pulled out Wilf's bag, passing it over the shoulder of a short, elderly man.

Wilf knew the man. His name was Tom Gonne, though people called him, 'Mayo Tom'.

Tom saw who was behind him, nodded and said in his kind way, 'Hello, Wilf. Drop round to our house later. Maureen has a scarf for you.'

Wilf nodded back. Maureen was Tom's wife.

He left with the bag, which was heavy. Jim was a generous man when he decided to give. That's what his mum always said, before adding, 'Just figure out the right days.'

At home, he spread the bag's contents on his kitchen table.

There was a blob of tripe, mutton cubes turning green, bones with shreds of flesh, liver, a packet of pork-and-leek sausages, and a tubular beef marrow bone chopped in half to expose the meat.

He was puzzled by the sausages. He unwound their wrapping and examined them. Why had they been included?

He brought them to his nose and sniffed. They were fresh. He wondered if they'd fallen to the floor.

But sausages were good, so he lifted one out, pulling more on a string, and took a bite.

It was flavoursome with leek. And peppery.

He finished it and ate another before putting them aside.

He thought now about what to give his fox first, and how to let the animal know the giver of the gift.

He decided on tripe, followed by the liver, then mutton and bones.

He found a solution to the identity question too. He fetched an old beanie, worn through winter. It kept his ears warm while he slept. It had grown mouldy from too much wear and emitted a meek pong.

He packed the tripe into it, squelching it side to side for osmosis. Then he returned everything to his plastic bag.

It occurred to him that if he needed to self-odorise fox food each time, Maureen's scarf might be useful.

It would be dark in a few hours. Darkness was bedtime.

8

NEXT day, being Saturday, he had no *Metro* round. He went to the wild cemetery with his tripe and beanie. He planned to leave the headwear as a memento working on his fox's subconscious.

He felt no need to rush. Foxes are nocturnal. If he'd seen it in daylight, it must have been agonised by hunger.

He roamed on some of the dirt tracks around the picturesque tombs, looking at angels, urns and four sepoys sculpted over the sarcophagus of a Raj General. He stopped by a plinth with a statue of a girl trying to look sad but restraining a giggle. Beyond it, he saw a tall young man staring at a Victorian grave.

Wilf knew him as the poet who lived in Number 3. It was one of the numbers on his *Metro* route. The poet made a living as a podcaster, Felicia told him, but Wilf had no idea of what a podcaster did. Nor did Felicia.

The poet was a graveyard regular who always came to the same grave. Wilf found him scary, a sort of crackpot, like old people who sat daily at their spouses' graves, whispering. People shouldn't visit graves at all, he felt. He had no idea why the poet haunted this one, but now had an urge to find out.

The young man heard him wading through the weeds, and turned a still-boyish face, with a reddish fizz of moustache.

'Hey, bud,' he said. 'Are you okay?'

'Is it your ancestors?'

'Here, no way. It's a teen who died in 1855 and was buried alone.'

He pointed at the inscription. 'Born 1841. Looks like her family built a memorial and forgot about her. They must be buried somewhere else.'

'What's she to you?'

'I'm trying to write about her. Visualise her. Can't crack it.'

Wilf felt gratified to have his idea of crackpotism proved right. The poet really was strange, though normal people accepted him.

'My ancestors are buried in Dublin, Belfast and Sligo,' droned the poet, confirming another of Wilf's ideas: poets drone.

'I knew you were Irish. I heard it in the voice.'

'What's the Irish voice like?'

'Made for graveyards.'

The poet laughed, making his face seem more boyish. 'Slick one-liner, bud.'

'And you can't pronounce the sound *th*. Good day to you.'

Wilf waded off again but the poet wasn't finished.

'Felicia says your mam was Irish.'

'Hrymmphh.'

He headed away to the thicket to make his offering.

He knew a secret about the poet. He was charitable like the Vicar. The poet sometimes stuffed some money through Wilf's letterbox. He didn't know Wilf had seen him, from a window upstairs. They were small amounts, a fiver, a tenner. 'To get love, you give love,' his mum chanted. Love meant gifts. Wilf pondered as he walked, did he need to give a gift back?

There were other things about the poet he knew, bad things, but Felicia told him never to tell or think about bad things.

9

IN the thicket he crept near to the spot where he'd seen the fox disappear. He knew he could leave meat anywhere and the fox would find it, as well as rats from the nearby canal. But shoving it under a thick bush shielded it from crows, of which dozens would otherwise swarm.

It was a gift in his new pet's home.

He felt fulfilment in putting it down. The thicket was rough, he had to get low, crouch, reach his hand out to shove briars away, catching his skin on barbs. Looking up. Quiet, shapely leaves, all different. He saw gravestones weedy and tilting, he felt something under his knee, hard. It was a stone heart with fading red paint, reading either Dad or Nan. He pushed the food further into the bush and backed away.

And afterwards, he was animated, ready for new things. He

walked for over an hour in a wide circle, taking in the Avenues around the sports centre. On arrival back in Yew Road, he went to Mayo Tom and Maureen's house, Number 43. He rang the bell.

'Wilf,' said Maureen, opening the door. 'I'm glad you came. Are you okay?'

'Tom said you had a scarf.'

'I do and it's warm, he's had it for years. I bought him a new one.'

'Thanks.'

'No, no, I know what you want. You want to take it and walk away. You'll step inside here first and have a cup of tea.'

He had hung back at the gate, feeling a strong impulse to flee. But with an effort of will he allowed her to escort him into a neat living room, where he sat at a table while she went to the kitchen to boil the kettle. She was even smaller than Tom, with a berry-shaped face and grey permed hair.

'Tom,' she said, through the open door, 'is at his computer. He's got into social media so does what his age group do. Asks who remembers the real Mayo?'

She emerged with a small tray that she placed on the table.

'Keeps him active. Now, will you have a few biscuits?'

There was a side plate of chocolate Hobnobs on the tray beside the mug of tea, spoon and a sugar bowl. Wilf began helping himself.

'You carry on. I'll pack the scarf.'

He consumed all the biscuits, while blowing on his tea to cool it. He never took sugar. The room was small but comfy, with a nurse's diploma on the wall and a vintage photo of a rural town, probably in Mayo. There was also a model aircraft on the sideboard, a Mosquito bomber, presumably Tom's handiwork.

He heard a binging noise from the kitchen as he finally gulped his tea. Maureen emerged with a bag that she placed on the table. He knew it held the scarf plus more and, as if waiting for a Flake, knew patience would be rewarded.

'You must have been hungry,' she said. 'Tell me, love, are you looking after yourself?'

'I'm fine.'

'You know if you ever want to come for a meal or a bit of a wash, you're always welcome.'

'I'm fine.'

'You've been a long time now, living on your own, haven't you?'

'Hrymmphh.'

'Okay.' After a pause she said, 'Well, you were never a talker. You don't do the tittle-tattle and good for you. Now old Tom up there can talk the ears off a donkey, and don't get him started on politics.'

'Politics,' said Wilf contemptuously.

'I agree. I think MPs should be forced to live on welfare a year before they're allowed to sit in that Parliament. Then, they'd know what it's like.'

Wilf said nothing more.

'Listen, I've microwaved a bit of rice and chicken and it's in the bag here wrapped in foil. If you eat it inside about an hour, it'll still be warm.'

Wilf nodded and took the bag. As he was leaving, he remembered something and turned back.

'Thanks,' he said.

He felt the side of the bag as he walked along the street. It was gently warm. He felt warm too. He'd talked to people today, not once, but twice. He was jubilant and excited, the two best feelings in life.

10

BUT the real excitement came later, after midnight.

He ate his rice and chicken before taking the scarf out of its tissue. It was soft blue wool, with a label saying, 'Foxford Woollen Mills'. He held it up with one hand, judging its length. After undoing his trousers, he draped one side down his left leg and one down his right, then redid his trousers. The scarf fringes were visible below the hems, on his shoes, but the wool nestled agreeably against his skin. After a few days of walking in it, there would be a fine osmosis.

For his evening routine, he rooted among his newspapers, choosing a copy of the *Independent* from a pile held down by a clothes rack. It was dated January 5th, 1998. The paper was yellow but easy to read. It had a report on a police dog crisis. Barking was in breach of new health-and-safety laws, but instead of charging dogs with an offence, their dog handlers were forced to wear ear plugs. They were punished for their dogs' crime.

Wilf laughed aloud. Discoveries like this were why newspapers were worth reading.

He was browsing art reviews in the Culture section as light faded and he went to the back bedroom to lie down. He drifted to sleep.

Loud noises woke him.

Opening the window, he saw a party in full swing two houses down. It had spilled out into the garden. Doors and windows had been flung wide open and music pounded into the night.

He recognised the tall figure of Ana the Czech, in a catsuit with laced sides revealing that beneath was nothing else. He heard voices speak in Czech and English, saw a vicar in a wicker chair tilt a vodka bottle to his lips, saw a bishop lean his crozier against the garden wall and chitchat to a woman in a tight dress starting mid-breast and ending mid-buttock. It wasn't just an engagement party. It was a whores & clerics engagement party.

The music was turned up a notch and more people spilled out to dance. Czech pop. The crowd swirled, with Czech girls belting out lyrics and British girls mouthing along. The bishop lost his mitre.

Suddenly into the midst of it all danced Felicia, in fishnet stockings. She danced with her fists, pumping the air to the beat.

Seeing that, Wilf had to dance too. He began punching the air and twirling on the spot. He did a two-step, a forward-back, knee bends and hip swings. In his dark room he got down and dirty to Czech pop.

11

HE woke next morning with a hangover, despite no alcohol. There was a dull throb at the side of his head. As he ate his cornflakes, his hand felt heavy holding the spoon.

The Skoda was still there when he went to feed the pigeons, but now he threw the flakes on the ground. The birds got to it anyway.

He had already decided not to feed his fox today. He reasoned if he fed it too much, it would stay selfish and vicious. Feed it just under enough, it would learn to respect him.

Nor did he feel like exercising, but Sundays saw his regular fitness routine. He always walked to Little Venice, at a brisk pace, an hour each way, cutting through the cemetery and out the gate by the Dissenters' Chapel, along the canal towpath, past the geese, down to the Venetian barges, stop, turn on the spot, back again.

So, he forced himself out, like every Sunday. It took an effort to trudge to the corner of Yew Road. As he turned at the ball court, he saw a guy from . . . Wilf couldn't remember where from, but not Britain. The guy lay on a bench, trying to lever himself up. Mario was his name but locals called him Supine Mario because he so often knocked himself out with powders, vapours and liquids.

Mario had a thrust of energy, as if by injection. He leapt upright, pointing at Wilf's feet.

'Wha's . . . 's, my man, Wilfie?'

Wilf glanced down and realised this was about the fringes of wool dangling below his trouser hems.

'Wha's, Wilfie?'

'What?'

'That blue?'

'It's my scarf.'

On the spur of the moment, Wilf swung around and walked home. He could hear Mario stumble after him a short way, saying, 'Wilfie, 's'okay, man.' He was audibly sobering.

When Wilf got indoors, he went straight upstairs to lie down. He really did not feel well. And outside lay ambushes.

12

He stayed in, slept sooner and longer than normal. When he woke, he could tell the time by the light on his wall. A fractured pattern radiated through plastic bags covering a broken windowpane. After so many years, he read it like a sundial.

His head was back to normal, though one of his cheeks felt numb. It was Monday. He needed to plan the week ahead.

He'd found a pet. He was no longer alone. He needed to understand.

He lingered, sitting on the side of his bed, reasoning.

'Always think in the mornings,' his mum used to say, 'before the day swallows you up.'

He thought about pets. Living creatures were long term. Foxes took longer, they were wild. Forging a link was harder to do. He must somehow change into a human that the animal instinctually trusted. He must be different, in many ways, in all ways.

But how could he be different?

He looked around him. The room was filled with newspapers, bags, and junk that he'd found on the streets. Too much, his house couldn't hold any more. He was forced to walk on little trails through mountainous piles.

He thought about people.

Could he force himself to speak to more? Overcome his fears of them? Build human bonds at the same time as with his fox, be socially acceptable?

'You say some crazy shit, Wilf,' said Felicia at times, 'but when you say nothing, you're fucking creepy.'

People. After his cornflakes and *Metro* round, he could choose his fox's feeding spots. Then try to talk to someone.

People might turn into a replacement routine. Even if they didn't change him, they would give him something to do.

13

A few hours later he was in the cemetery. He brought the liver in one of his old socks.

He scouted in the most neglected zones. There were dense brambles by the thicket, too thorny even for foxes. Rubbish obscured the canal wall and a spinney grew at the junction of two dirt tracks. A robin perched and he watched it until it flew away.

He decided to leave food at the base of a tree near a Nobel prize-winner's grave. Since vertical, Wilf wondered if the tree was logically above or beyond the skeleton laureate? Harold Pinter. His fox would never win prizes or go to Sweden but would find the food and smell Wilf's scent.

He also scouted dropping points at the O'Hagan mausoleum and near the West Gate. Gradually, he would lure the animal home.

Happy with himself, but nervous, he went to find someone to talk to.

14

THE day was sunny and hot. A lot of people were outdoors. Football was being played in the ball court while in the playground smaller kids slid, swung, or clambered. Supine Mario was back on his bench, downing cans of Polish beer alongside a guy on crutches and a drunk woman with a scab on her lip.

'Wilfie,' said Mario. But Wilf ignored him.

On the Birch Road bench by the parking meter were another

group, also drinking. Big Don Jones was holding court, with his soldierly hair, bulging midriff and oyster eyes. Wilf heard him talk about the Chelsea midfield, Brexit, and bringing back the death penalty, but could rarely blend disparate ideas. He knew those on this bench felt superior to those on Mario's bench.

Nobody acknowledged him as he lingered, but he walked off when a few stares began to take aim.

He was back on Yew Road when he saw Professor Emma, taking the sun outside her home. She was a history lecturer at Southbank University. She was reading a book, holding it close to her sunglasses. Her legs were proudly tanning in a summer dress that spread colourfully against her wheelchair.

The professor had been nearly killed by a motorbike on Harrow Road. When she came out of rehab, sad and devastated in a chair, Wilf began delivering *Metros* to her in the mornings. He knew she liked to read. 'To get love, you give love,' chanted his mum. Wilf wanted to show love because he wasn't able to express himself in the sympathetic words her other neighbours used so easily.

'Never say sorry, Wilf,' his mum often said. 'You are who you are.'

Other people had said 'sorry' to Emma, but he couldn't.

He was thinking of this, swaying forward and back, when she became aware of him, a few metres away.

'Wilf. Are you okay? You look like you're stalking me.'

She raised her dark glasses on little hinges, revealing clear normal glass beneath. She surveyed his clothes, down to the blue wool fringes.

'Flamboyant! Reminds me of something I wore at Glastonbury Festival. Van Morrison played and the Pyramid stage burnt down.'

She paused as if waiting for a reply, which never came.

'Yeah,' she resumed. 'I liked floaty clothes and was into braids.'

Wilf stayed quiet. He didn't know what to say. He wanted to speak, but no words came into his mind.

'Are you in a sulk? You haven't snorted once.'

'Good day to you, Emma,' said Wilf, about to turn away.

'Don't be stroppy. I saw you looking at my book. It's historical fiction. Real bolus of barf.'

'I read newspapers.'

'Me too. The *Metro* every morning. Wilf, listen, why don't you take one of my books? I have too many and I was going to send boxes to charity shops.'

'I don't read books.'

'Suit yourself, then.'

Wilf walked a few steps away but then stopped and turned back. 'I'll read a book.'

'Go in and choose one,' said Emma, gesturing to her open door.

Wilf walked up the ramp and heard the purr of her electric chair following. Her house was open plan, with a chair lift on the stairs. He spotted a second manual wheelchair at the top. Books were everywhere, even littering the stairs. One entire wall was stocked to the ceiling. Wilf deduced Emma didn't intend to read the highest ones again. Destined for the boxes.

'I have one condition,' said Emma. 'Make coffee. Over there, the kitchen unit. The kettle.'

'Pour water in.'

'It's in already. Just click down the button at the back.'

He did so and gargling heating noises erupted.

'Go get your book while it boils. I have more upstairs. But don't touch anything about Eleanor of Aquitaine.'

Wilf realised there was a time limit. Abruptly he rushed upstairs, taking care not to brush the second wheelchair. The door to the back room was wide open. The bed had rumpled coverings and a rail. It was where she slept. The other two doors were shut. He opened both, finding rooms with no furnishings.

He went back to her bedroom and looked at more stacks. This room had a mirrored dresser, a wall plasma screen, laptop, desk, and wardrobe. He looked at book spines. Finally, a thick green spine caught his eye, midway down a pile. He prised it out carefully, holding his arm against the higher ones. Then rushed downstairs.

'Show,' said Emma. 'Oscar Wilde biography. Good choice.'

Just then, the kettle stopped boiling with a click.

'Cups are in the cupboard under, I can't reach high. I want to get rid of the books up there,' pointing at the wall. 'They're crap.'

Wilf leaned over the cupboard and took out two mugs.

'Coffee in that jar there. Spoon in the drawer. Milk in the fridge. Sugar in the jar with the Tinkerbell fairy on it.'

'I don't take sugar.'

'I take two, thanks. Put a spoonful of coffee in both cups, pour in water, put in milk, then do what you like. But two spoonfuls.'

Wilf followed her instructions. He handed her a mug. But instead of concentrating on his own, he took up the Tinkerbell jar and started to shake it.

'What are you doing?'

'You dip wet spoons in sugar,' explained Wilf. 'Makes it hard at the bottom. Loosen it for you.'

'Whatever Wilf does, he does for a reason,' said Emma, referring to him in the third person, as many did.

15

BACK home, he felt tired and barely glanced at his new book, except to notice from photos on the sleeves that Oscar Wilde needed a haircut.

He lay down and drifted into a long sleep. He dreamt again of the two willows over his mum's grave. The fox, which by now had evolved speech, squeezed out. It said that living in holes was nobody's preference, but rents were harsh on foxes, and his mum was juicy company. It spoke just like Professor Emma, but in an animal's voice.

Its voice woke him up.

It was Tuesday.

In fact, it was Torture Tuesday. The worst of all days.

'Moanday, Tearsday, Woesday,' chanted his mum, 'don't days have funny names, Wilf?'

Torture Tuesday was a day every two weeks when he had to sign on as unemployed. In British law, people with no work had to endure torture in a building called Jobcentre Plus. These had been called Jobcentres once, until law turned more hostile and added Plus for 'plus suffering'.

It was his least favourite routine, but the only one that always got him a little cash. Less than £50 a week.

As usual he arrived early.

Jobcentre Plus was a roomy, three-tiered building, where the ground floor had job noticeboards and computer screens, the second held torture cubicles, and the third held administrative offices. Wilf lingered looking at jobs. He saw a role as a samosa folder in Alperton, and a palette handler in Park Royal.

When his time came, he was admitted to the second floor and directed to a far open-backed cubicle. He felt eyes watching him from all around. Some people began shifting from their seats. It could only mean one thing – a new staff member. All new staff members were assigned to him.

A stranger was waiting, with a desk plate named, 'Andrew Shaw, Work Coach.'

'Wilf Kelly?'

'Hrymmphh,' said Wilf, handing over his job hunt record. This was a booklet where he had to write down all the jobs he'd applied for in the past fortnight. Wilf scribbled illegibly in it every few days.

One of Andrew's eyebrows was hyperactive and squirmed as he tried to decipher the script. Wilf noticed some of Andrew's colleagues drift to a water cooler and desks behind him.

'What sort of work are you looking for, Mr Kelly?'

'Samosas. Palettes.'

'Samosas?'

'I can fold.'

Andrew's eyebrow upturned. He scrolled through Wilf's file on his computer screen.

'You've been unemployed since . . . 1989. On disability allowance till 2015. You were called in for a Work Capability Assessment?'

Wilf said nothing, despite the questioning tone.

'And declared . . . fit to work?'

'I'm not disabled,' said Wilf, thinking of Emma.

'Where did you look for work in the last fortnight?'

'Supermarkets.'

'Which ones?'

'The one on the Grove.'

'Where have you been looking in recent years?'

'Supermarkets.'

'For example?'

'The one on the Grove. Every week.'

'You ask for a job in the same supermarket every week?'

'They said something could turn up any time.'

'The one you were fired from?'

'Hrymmphh.'

Andrew's face was like a tortoise being fed plastic lettuce leaves. More people glided behind him. Among them was Shaunda, the manager, who had a sly grin. Wilf recalled a news piece he read in a *Daily Mirror* once. It was about a torturer who signed interrogation reports with a smiley face.

'It says here you don't have a bank account.'

'I don't like banks.'

'You need a bank account to get Universal Credit payments.'

'I have a card,' said Wilf, brandishing his card.

'That's a Payment Exception Card. For emergencies. It's temporary.'

'So are we,' responded Wilf. 'So was my mum.'

'Your *mum*? Mr Kelly. There are things we can help with, but . . . I can't believe you're seriously looking for work. I'm sorry, I have no choice. By law, I have to suspend your benefits.'

His colleagues were now shaking, trying to laugh silently. Wilf raised his hand towards Shaunda, who unperched her rump from a desk. She ambled over and gave Andrew a tap. He became aware of noise and, as he glanced back, his colleagues let themselves rip.

'Andy,' said Shaunda. 'Wilf's been suspended by every one of us on our first day here. It's why we start newcomers on Tuesdays.'

She put her hand reassuringly on his shoulder, 'Wilf's our secret mascot, aren't you, Wilf?'

'My money,' said Wilf, loudly.

'Don't worry. Go to Spar tomorrow with your card and they'll give it to you.' She was breaking into a grin again. 'Bye, Wilf. Take care.'

Wilf stood up. 'And love the freaky trousers.'

'Good day to you, Shaunda.'

He left. The torture was over.

16

WHEN Shaunda herself had suspended Wilf from benefits four years ago, Felicia had visited the Jobcentre to seek her out. She explained that Wilf couldn't cope with work, or application forms.

'I thought so,' said Shaunda. 'I felt bad. He should still be on disability.'

'He's vulnerable.'

'I'll find workarounds,' promised Shaunda, who was a good-humoured woman from Harlesden. 'I won't force him onto any stupid courses. Fuck the rules.'

'Fuck the rules, sis,' echoed Felicia.

But the day wasn't all torture.

That afternoon, Wilf stood outside his house, beside his gatepost that tilted at a ten-degree angle. Felicia came over to coax him and a bag of laundry into her home, where hot food and a shower waited. He left his scarf behind, to preserve its odour.

Felicia, of course, had already noticed it, and gently pointed out that scarves were for necks, not trousers.

'Keeps me warm,' said Wilf.

'It's summer.'

'Keeps me warm,' repeated Wilf.

'Jesus, love,' said Felicia trying to hold in laughter. 'Poor old Maureen will think she's turned you into a pervert.'

Later, he read his book, in the long summer evening. It was published in 1989 by Hamish Hamilton. The biographer, Richard Ellmann, was Goldsmiths' Professor of English Literature at Oxford until 1984. It had illustrations. One caught his eye. It was a drawing that read, 'Lady Wilde ("Speranza"), painted by J. Morosini.'

It reminded him of something.

He remembered the Celtic cross beside his fox's thicket. He'd glimpsed its inscription, to someone called Speranza. He must go and look at it again.

But then he would be haunting a grave, like the poet from Number 3. Crackpot behaviour.

He was drifting asleep again. He closed the biography of Wilde and curled up, as twilight spun its patterns past the plastic bag dial.

His head hurt a bit. He felt like sleeping until his life changed.

17

WHEN he woke next morning, it hit him with force that everything had – permanently – changed.

Till now his days were congested with routines. But he couldn't keep doing the same things anymore.

Wednesday was his favourite day. It was Council bin day where, as well as bins, people left unwanted stuff outside. Sometimes they perched items on their garden walls. Broken kettles were a regularity. He often had to walk many streets to find something interesting. Then he would take out one of his bags, if small, or manually lift and carry larger items off.

In this way he hoarded dead lamps, console tables and stools dotted in his home, buried under other stuff. Mostly, he found nothing. Or a few newspapers, to add to his reading trove. Or a miscellany: dolls, routers, baskets, staplers, ring binders, vases, dinky cars, a toy dinosaur, hundreds similar. Now tangled in seemingly senseless clutter but clumped in codes infusing instincts of belonging and asylum. Making it home.

When he found clothes, it was a special experience. He would stretch an item out and hold it over a part of his body to check if it would fit. To him, colours, combinations, materials, never mattered. He once wore a puce-and-yellow waistcoat and cargo pants that left kids hooting with derision, until Felicia told him he looked like a bad painting, which, by experience, she knew was exactly the right criticism. He threw the waistcoat away.

The only things he wouldn't bring home were books, though there were plenty to be found on the streets, outside gates or on garden walls.

But his mum had died reading a book, which was why he avoided them. He'd found her in bed in the front bedroom. He knew that the last page she read was thirty-nine, its number visible on a corner, though he didn't know her last word. The book was still there, in the bedroom. Its glue had blistered, and pages spilled from its covers. It was called *The Birds*, but its associations didn't make him dislike birds, with the exception of crows.

He remembered her body. Her nostrils were wider and darker. It was her only difference from life. It was a confusing morning because he had to ring Felicia's doorbell and allow men into the house to take her away. Anger followed confusion, and he lost his job quickly. Felicia had tried to persuade him not to go to work. But it was routine. What else was he to do?

A week later, he watched other men lower her coffin into a hole. Then felt Felicia tugging him away.

Now he had a new book. Oscar Wilde.

How much time would it fill? Or would Wilde slowly disinter his mum? He tried not to think about it.

There was also his fox. Today was a feeding day and he decided to use the O'Hagan mausoleum, which had shrub cover around its foundations. But that wouldn't take long.

He needed to think out the right routines, to fill time.

He would go to Spar, to get his money. Then, like every other payday, he would go to the fish-and-chip shop to spend the first £1.50. The Portuguese woman behind the counter would spread a white sheet of paper, and pile two scoops of chips on it. 'More,' he'd say. 'Don't be greedy,' she'd warn, shaking the scooper at him before scooping more.

He would reach over the counter with the saltshaker and season the hot chips. He never took vinegar.

'Pare, wait,' she'd say. Then she'd pop something on his chips for free – a saveloy, a pie, a piece of fried chicken or, his favourite, a few strips of kebab meat. She would conclude by wrapping the food and putting it in a carrier bag, giving it to him with a glimpse of smiling eyes.

But eating didn't take long.

He realised days were filled with too much time.

People. Everything came back to people. They still clogged him with dread. They reinforced his sensation of not knowing what to say. How could he change?

An idea came to him.

He could expand his *Metro* round. Recruit more people who wanted a daily paper delivered.

18

Of all his routines, the *Metro* round was best. The one that gave his life the most stability.

It started one morning in the 1990s as he walked past the train station.

He saw two tall bins with sides cut away. In them were hundreds of copies of a newspaper called *Metro*, with the word FREE emblazoned on it.

He took up a bundle to take home, then put them back and took just one. He only needed one to read.

But as weekdays went by and he saw new *Metros*, he felt uncomfortable neglecting the unread. They were free. Why didn't people want them?

An idea came to him. He invented a new routine.

He took an armful of *Metros* and walked around the tree streets. if he saw a car belonging to someone he knew, and who didn't scare him, he left a *Metro* under the windscreen wiper.

He did it every day.

One car belonged to a man now long dead. It was a restored '70s Ford Capri. The man was a former stand-up comedian, a gaunt kinky-haired guy with prominent cheekbones, whose vocal cords had been operated on because of throat cancer. He caught Wilf one morning putting the *Metro* on his car.

He came close, with fingers pressed to his neck, to activate his soundbox.

'Know how hard 's drive with a newspaper?' he said, in his whisper.

'I don't drive.'

'Put it through me door. No charge.'

'Number 16.'

'Cut ads out first.'

'I don't cut ads, too many.'

"S censoring mankind's right to sell. World's biggest crime.'

Wilf and he stood looking at each other a moment.

''S'alright, I'm only jokin'. Nothin' to say, Wilf?'

'Hrymmphh.'

'That's what I like to hear.'

Then the comedian got into his car and drove away with the *Metro* still under the wiper.

19

THE next day, Felicia asked for a home delivery too. Then, more people asked. Word got around and even Wilf, who was seldom aware of networking, knew the comedian was behind it. It was why the gaunt man's funeral was the only one he ever went to after his mum's, standing behind everyone else, hands in pockets.

Over the years, he developed the rule of delivering a *Metro* only to those who asked. Apart from Professor Emma, the exception was newcomers for whom, if they had a car, he left a welcoming *Metro* under the wiper. He even left one for Ana, who fooled him by not having Czech number plates, but now she was a regular. Frostbitten mornings or birdsong dawns, he delivered, at times even waiting at the train station for the delivery van.

The recipients and route varied over time. But someone always wanted to know the news.

It gave purpose to his days.

He had a dozen on his route now, including a few who still made him shy, like the poet and Ana, but others less so - like Felicia, Emma, Luca the Frenchman, Norris's mum, Beardy Callum, Island Garth, Ray who wrote for the *Times* and the three Toms.

They were all nice to him, and often thanked him.

Some liked to have their bell rung when he arrived. Beardy Callum, who had a torrential growth to his chest, frequently opened his door in dresses black or blue, cut to the knee. Island Garth was glad of a chance to escape his wife a few moments and often invited him in for fried fish (which he declined, though it smelt nice). Ray who wrote for the *Times* sometimes opened his door as Wilf approached and slipped him a little money with a nod of his head and nothing said.

He rarely saw Norris's mum, who walked with a stick. Norris had been transferred from Wormwood Scrubs to Huntercombe Prison. It added hours to her visits. Wilf saw her limping now and then, sticked and in a high-collared blouse, towards the train station. She had given birth late.

20

His greatest joy was to deliver to the three Toms, who appealed to his sense of humour.

The three – all called Tom – lived next door to each other at Numbers 41, 43 and 45 Yew Road. The neighbourhood distinguished them as English Tom, Mayo Tom, and Bulfast Tom. The last was from Belfast but couldn't pronounce the name of his home city.

They were long-time residents who, after camaraderie springing from discovering a name in common, grew to hate each other. Anger erupted from solid, if casual, affronts (such as English Tom labelling Bulfast Tom's wife a Filipina mail-order bride), then mutated into a clinging fog of revulsions, with more and more offences added, leading to a point where none of the Toms left their homes without first checking that the coast was clear.

This meant Wilf's delivery – the last on his round – had an epilogue. He always left the *Metro* on the Toms' doorsteps and took up a seat on the low wall of one of the houses opposite.

Normally the wives, Maureen or Maja, emerged. English Tom was a widower. They sometimes came out at the same time and would nod, or chat, or wave over to Wilf. English Tom, who still lusted after women, and noticed things from his window, would also come out, say, 'Morning', and take his news, gawping at the wives.

But rarely – just rarely – two of the Toms would come out and see each other. Their faces were worth the wait.

Wilf got a lot of private laughter from this. Sometimes, even on bad nights when he was freezing and staring at moonlit flitters on the wall, he thought of the three Toms and grinned.

21

FELICIA, who knew just about everyone on the tree streets, said to Maja one day,

'Wilf really believes they hate each other.'

'Easy to fool, uh?'

'Do they choreograph?'

'Hey, where you think I'm from? English school? What that mean?'

'Oh, never mind,' said Felicia. 'Keeps him happy.'

'Wilf's okay,' said Maja. 'In his own world, uh?'

But today's *Metro* round left Wilf feeling dissatisfied.

Nobody emerged from any of the three Toms' homes and, after sitting for fifteen minutes, he left with a sense of void.

In the graveyard, he pushed aside shrubs at the O'Hagan tomb and hid another old sock with mutton cubes. He lingered for a while sitting on the wall of the De Lissa tomb, on the lookout for thieving crows.

Then he left dutifully to find more people to recruit for the *Metro* round.

If he saw someone on the street, he slowed. But saw no one he knew. Dread still clung to him.

He ranged so far, he found himself on streets he always avoided.

He was on Chamberlayne Road, where he saw a line of roofs with turrets and gables. His mind seemed to spiral. He sensed himself as if from above standing in mismatched clothes on a kerbside, exposed.

Chamberlayne was different now. It had new shops. New colours. Tidier. He'd walked it daily as a child to school on the corner. He never came back anymore.

There was a display of oranges outside the old public toilet, built by Victorians in 1893. It had been turned into a trendy café with an Italian flag flying. He pictured it as it was before, a tiled isolated building, with two gates, saying, 'Gents' and 'Ladies'.

He walked up to the oranges, piled loosely on a two-wheeled cart with poles leaning on the ground, as if waiting for a horse. He felt an impulse to pick up the poles and run the cart away. Instead, he plucked out an orange that was turning green with fungus and threw it to the ground.

When he looked up, he saw a man in the café watching him. He put his head down and strode away.

It felt like school. People scaring him. Except Felicia who walked him home most days and defended him.

22

HE was manoeuvring miserably to his house when, on Beech Road, he saw Luca the Frenchman walking towards him, pushing his wheelbarrow. Sinewy in a sky-blue T-shirt and shorts, he looked like a beachcomber with a tan and hair more white than grey.

Wilf felt a surge of relief.

Luca was the tree streets' least scary man.

Luca hated shopping, so always bought groceries in bulk, at the supermarket on the Grove. He didn't have a car and groceries were heavy, so he took taxis home. After a while, he realised it was cheaper and healthier to invest in a wheelbarrow. So, every few weeks he wheeled home a cargo of supplies routinely.

Wilf waited for the Frenchman to come close.

'Is it heavy?' he was able to ask.

'Yes,' said Luca, lowering the barrow and rubbing his hands. 'But I'm stronger than I look. I started in my father's stockyard, lifting bags with cement.'

He had only a slight accent. Felicia said he'd gone to the Sorbonne, the best university in France.

'I don't get into fights,' Luca resumed. 'People laugh at me. I don't care. I'm a pacifist – do you know this word?'

'Don't fight.'

'Exactly. My uncle was a pacifist in his face. He led demos in '68. A gendarme hit him in the face with a baton. All his life, he wore pacifism in his face, you know, cheek broken.'

Wilf felt like he had been given a gift of communication.

'I was born in '71.'

'Good, good. I was born in '62. I'm older.' Luca paused, as if waiting for Wilf to engage again. He couldn't.

'How are you today, okay?'

'I'm fine.'

'I'm glad. We don't talk too much.'

'I don't like talking.'

'Ah, but you talk to Felicia. I see you all the time.'

Wilf didn't know what to say again. After a pause, Luca lifted his wheelbarrow and began to push forward.

'Never be a stranger.'

He carried on along the street at a rational pace.

Wilf remembered Felicia once saying, 'A Sorbonne man without a car means only one thing – he's bankrupt.'

Luca had a secret.

23

LUCA mentioned the chat when he ran into Felicia. She was pleased.

'He's coming out of his shell,' she said.

'It lasted five minutes,' said Luca. 'He didn't, you know, do that thing he does, the *hrrr . . . rrreh . . . reh*.'

'It's his multipurpose word, it can mean anything.'

Luca nodded. 'He'd fit naturally into a French philosophy department, then.'

By Thursday, a full week had passed since he'd met his fox.

During that time, he had abandoned picking things up, gone into Emma's and Maureen's homes, started conversations with the poet and Luca the Frenchman, and chosen a book. Pets were transformational.

At the same time, glints of fear lingered. Changes to routines were like flailing skin, stripping it off and covering the wounds with makeshift grafts. He knew that these would need time to blend, be smoothed. Day after day.

He felt this fear accounted for his dull headache. It had begun to come back, and persist, then go away again.

Since today was an anniversary, he decided to overfeed his fox. A stench from the marrow, strong even by his tolerance, also convinced him it was time to get rid of the bones.

Using his mum's old scissors, he cut strands from the fringes of Maureen's scarf. These he pressed into the meat of the two marrow bones, until they clung. He had other old clothes, but reasoned old clothes meant old scent. The scarf had a fresh, living scent. His fox would know he was real.

At the cemetery, he put one of the marrow bones under shrubs behind the HER statue. He left the other half in a bush near the West Gate.

After this, he walked in open space, on the wide, hay-grass expanse surrounding the writer Trollope's grave. He flung bones far and wide and powerfully as he could. He saw crows swoop, land, and poke, erupting in a tone of caw that must translate as 'eat'. Big and little stood off, and the biggest got forward to poke most, with other sneaky cheats bobbing back and forth, getting their beaks to shreds of flesh.

Crows had an orchestra of noises, but only one for eat.

After watching them, Wilf left the cemetery, steeling himself to the thought that he had to find more new routines.

24

ROUTINES were special. Each took patience, as if building a jigsaw or designing a mosquito bomber, neither of which he'd ever done, but whose principles he understood.

At times, Felicia tried to tempt him to break his habits. Meeting him in the street, with her two grandkids holding her hands, she said, 'We're going to London Zoo. Come on Wilf, come with us.'

'Uncle Worzel,' said little Vince Jr.

'Stop that,' said his grandmum.

Wilf was sorely tempted. His mum had brought him to London Zoo and he was mesmerised by its animals.

'Hrymmphh,' he said finally, towards Vince Jr.

He realised that Jim Lyon had given him too much meat for his fox. So, tweaking his newest routine, he took a small black off-licence bag with him today for more fox food. At closing time, he returned to collect it, with a sense of pleasure at its lighter load.

He did the same in the following weeks, still feeding his fox in the graveyard, prodding pieces of the blue scarf deep into the meat. It began getting shorter and soon nobody could spot any trace of it in his clothes.

Jim still put pork-and-leek sausages in the bag. But there was variety – kidneys, mince, chops.

It also began including a £5 note. It wasn't from Jim. If Jim gave, it would be big. It might be Pencil Ear.

Wilf was patient, drawing in the net. He reasoned that by the time he used all the wool of his scarf, his pet would be sitting in his kitchen.

25

OSCAR Wilde gave him a bigger problem. The book seemed to make his mum feel alive again.

She'd been a creature of routine too. She adored books but didn't like old stuff lying in her house. She bought books one at a time. When she finished one, she gave it to him. Then bought another. When she finished that, she would buy another, throw Wilf's book away and replace it with the one she'd just finished, before reading her new one.

'Wilf, catch up with me,' she said. 'Learn not to be a slow yoke, but a rapid little reader. Did you understand all the words?'

'What's amulet?' said Wilf.

'That means, like, a magic bracelet. Something that protects you against bad people.'

'Can I have one?'

'You have me, darling, you don't need an amulet.'

Because she read faster than him, Wilf rarely finished a book. But he never complained when it was taken away. There was another one to look forward to.

Books were like jigsaws too. He read from the middle, the end, blurbs, publishers, dates. Piecing it all together in his mind. He read Dickens, and Macken, and Larkin, and Salinger, while still a preteen. He was reading Auden while his mum died upstairs, reading *The Birds* by Tarjei Vesaas.

In a mix of grief and filial obedience, he threw Auden into the bin after her funeral, as she would have done.

So, reading Oscar Wilde shrouded him in complex emotions. He wondered if he should read it the same way as his mum, from beginning to end. Or read it in his own way, picking, poking, prodding. This was why he loved newspapers so much. Nobody read a newspaper from start to finish.

He decided to read it all, in his own way, at his own pace, a little each day, hopping forward and back, to put the jigsaw together.

It didn't take him long to decide Oscar would approve of this. And Speranza – whom he discovered to be Oscar's mum – would urge it. The Wildes had minds more like his.

He remembered the day he'd finished school, at the same time as Felicia. His mum invited her over to the house, where, in the back garden, Felicia and he put their remaining schoolbooks in a galvanised bucket. His mum poured lighter fuel over them, and they allowed Wilf to light the fire.

Smoke and flecks of ashen paper rose from the flames, and they felt their spirits find freedom like moths breaking from a chrysalis.

26

HIS hardest new routine was to find recruits for his *Metro* round.

He roamed the streets. He realised he didn't know many people anymore. Newcomers came and went. British newcomers had career paths, degrees, kids, mortgages, confidence. Foreign ones did menial jobs, like his mum's generation of Irish used to do, and some still did.

Over years, as if by attrition, familiar faces died or sold their homes. Where they'd disappeared, paint on the housefronts gleamed cleaner. Porch lights shone and scaffolding was erected by workers constructing attic dens. When doors opened, strangers with car fobs emerged.

The tree streets weren't as familiar as they used to be.

One afternoon, he turned onto Yew Road after a routine roam. He saw three of these strangers, all new to the area.

They were on their knees with gardening trowels. By the ball court wall was a line of plants with roots wrapped in nets. The strangers were digging in the soil border surrounding the court, which gave it a perimeter of trees, benches, earth, litter, and squirrels.

They'd put up a sign saying, 'Community Garden – Greening the Streets.'

It seemed to Wilf like a clear case of crackpotism and bad gardening.

His mum would have chosen to plant sensible potatoes, cabbage and thyme in that perimeter. Maybe a sweet pea trim against the wall, for brightness, and a few well-chosen flowering plants.

He shrank into resentment and stood swaying.

The woman of the group rolled her haunches back on her heels and looked at him. She had a pale face with large, blue eyes that seemed to bobble as they came to rest. She wore a stylish silver ring in her nose.

'Wanna join in?'

Her voice was rich, rasping and loudly sweet. He said nothing.

'You're Wilf, aren't you?' Felicia told me about you. She said green fingers run in your veins.'

'Are you a Yank?' he demanded.

'Texan. Eileeen with three 'e's. That's Marcus, he's a film restorer. Celluloid to digital. That's Oliver. He supports QPR.'

Oliver, a wiry man, rose.

'Somebody has to,' he explained.

He draped down resignedly planting lavender.

'Wilf,' asked Eileen, gesturing him closer and pointing at one of the bagged plants, 'Do you know what that is?'

'Hollyhock. Tap root. Dig deep or they die.'

'Can you help me plant it?'

'I don't dig.'

'You don't have to. Just hold it steady.'

'This space is a Council responsibility. We don't have to do it.'

'We've got permission. We *want* to.'

'Good day to you, Eileen,' said Wilf abruptly and walked away.

By the time he got to between Numbers 3 and 5, he remembered something. He went back to Eileen as her head stooped and hand dug.

'I have an iris,' he said.

Eileen smiled.

'Get it, Wilf.'

Wilf did. He tore up Yew Road at his fastest stride. Home, he took a key out of his deep pocket, opened the door, didn't shut it, walked through the hall and kitchen, to his mum's garden, tended lovingly until her death.

It was now in ruin. Her pear tree was twisted and writhing, drowning in bindweed and cat smells. There were nettles. Weeds were monstrous. Vegetables were extinct.

He never came out, except on a routine each 13th. But knew exactly where to look. She'd taught him well.

He'd helped her plant an iris beside a mint.

'Some plants never die, Wilf,' she said. 'Iris never dies, mint always grows.'

A mint bush was still there, green and lush, unperturbed by overgrowth. At its shoulder, the tall green blades of an iris wilted but persisted.

Wilf fetched a bread knife. He sawed its blade into the tuber, cutting and twisting a piece from the soil. He knew the iris would survive assault and next year issue purple flowers.

He yanked up the last strands and hurried out, making sure his door was secure. He brought it to Eileen, still digging, looking sweaty.

'Here,' he said.

'No, there.' She pointed her trowel to a spot with a trench already dug.

He showed her how to lay the tuber in and touched her hand

to stop her piling on too much soil. It was a nice moment, but as he stood up, he knew he was too shy to ask the strangers about the *Metro*. He abruptly walked away.

'Wilf,' she called, 'Will you water it?'

'Hrymmphh.'

'Yeh, walk off,' she snorted back. 'Y'all do the same thing too when you make us pregnant.'

Wilf knew he hadn't made her pregnant. But it surprised him and made him look back. She was digging with her trowel, as if for oil rather than petals.

27

'Did he take the bait?' asked Felicia, calling round to her new friend Eileen's house that evening with a bottle of wine.

'Sort of. He brought us a cutting. Hey, I love the way you guys pull around him, it's so full-on British. And he sort of looks like, ah . . .'

'I know. So, is he going to help with the garden?'

'No.'

'Shit,' said Felicia. 'I really thought he might get into it. He spent a lot of time with his mum in their garden. He was eager.'

'I tried my best,' said Eileen. 'Mea no fucking culpa.'

Wilf kept wandering the streets, every day feeling the need to reach out. When he recognised people, all he could manage to say was, 'Hrymmphh'. Mostly, he passed strangers.

After a while, it didn't matter anymore. It grew into a new love of dawdling. He began to forget his original reasons. He found himself suddenly happy, being alone.

Truly, deeply.

What did anything matter anymore?

Sometimes he stood still on a street, to spot birdlife, mostly pigeons. Sometimes he said something to nobody. As he passed the Persian restaurant on Harrow Road, its baker who worked long hot hours spreading dough in a rotund oven stopped him and gave him a bag of flatbreads. He patted Wilf's shoulder and said words in Persian. Wilf understood the meaning to be kind. The breads were in a bag with interior foil lining, and some were wrapped around warm lamb mince.

Each day, as light faded, he stood on Harrow Road. He watched for parakeets flying to their roosts in the cemetery. They flew in green squadrons, spaced out. Like military jets, single-minded, never colliding. It was the only time he ever heard parakeets stay silent, except for an occasional air-command squawk, which veered their direction.

He saw a magpie fly vertically, from a sill to the gutter above. The bird was as slovenly as an industrial elevator but rose just as straight.

At ground level he saw Big Don Jones, also slovenly, a shirt wing untucked. His eyes looked more and more like oysters, resting in a shell of salt water. He seemed to have taken to the streets too, and frequently Wilf found himself sharing the pavement, at which point he crossed the road or did a U-turn.

Something was wrong with Big Don. He was usually confident, cock-of-the-walk, the first one into an argument, pointing out what he alone knew. But Wilf knew his life was churning.

Don's mother had just died.

Wilf thought of trying to say, 'Sorry'. But Don was big enough and scary enough to feel unapproachable. He avoided him. Don reminded him of something his mum once said:

'People are a type of animal, Wilf.'

'Birds,' the little boy replied.

'Birds,' said his mum squeezing him. 'I think you're like a bird in a big orchard painting. Do you remember all the paintings we saw?'

'Colours.'

'What colours do you like?'

'Orange and yellow.'

'Are they bird or fruit colours?'

'Both.'

But if Big Don were a bird, he would be a crow. If he were a fruit, he would be a sour grape.

His mum felt so alive now. It felt like she was stepping out of Wilde's world every time he opened the book.

One evening, his eyes were caught by a yellow top, worn by a familiar young woman. She was one of the Carson twins. She stood at an array of fruit displayed outside the greengrocery, on the other side of the street, probing in boxes of mangos and plums, testing their ripeness.

The display was the glamour point of this stretch of Harrow Road. Amid the duns and dusty traffic, fruit in crates stood out shiny and linear. It reminded Wilf of a painting he'd seen by a foreigner called Mondrian.

He'd seen it in a book given to him by his mum. *Modern Painting*, by Phaidon. The book made a great impression. He stared at its pictures for hours, fascinated. He got through all the bright paintings, but not all the text, before she took it away and gave him a different book.

Susan Carson, swaying over the fruit stand, seemed to be conducting a Mondrian symphony of gridded colours. Though thin, she moved in shapes.

Wilf remembered his mum's shapes, as she leaned over him at mealtimes, or showed her hair silhouetted against a window. She liked to wear yellows, and greens, and plumpy jumpers of wild furry pink. From behind, she'd looked like Susan Carson.

28

AND Susan gave him a new idea.

He realised he could never grow his *Metro* round by roaming the streets. And roaming did not bring him closer to being normal, no matter how satisfying it felt at the time.

His new idea was to knock on doors where safe people, like Susan Carson, lived, to ask if they'd like to be added to his *Metro* round. He could go door to door, like a salesman, or meter reader, or pollster.

Knocking on doors was his final frontier. It meant waiting, listening for approaching sounds from inside, not knowing who exactly would answer, or how they would react to him.

But he could start with the softest target – Susan herself. The Carson household, where she lived with her twin brother.

He'd thought a few times of delivering to the twins, but always shrank back because the male, Paulie, was a friend of Big Don. He was part of his circle and would join Don in an unreadable stare if Wilf got too close.

But he had a different personality. Paulie sometimes tried to flick Wilf's ear if they passed on the street but would put a hand on his alarmed arm and say, 'Y'alright, Worzel?' calming him. He just liked clowning around.

Paulie had been a hard-living gas engineer for most of his adult life, swigging lagers till closing time in Maggie's Bar, then hitting the road each morning to fix gas boilers. But he was transfigured one day when a boiler erupted, smattering parts of his face with third-degree burns.

Susan was frail, pixie-like, always gossiping intently with friends. Not pretty, but pliable. A lot of men had worn a path before arriving elsewhere (and regretting it), leaving her with a prevalent air of neediness. Her biggest crush had been Norris, who she still visited in prison. Her head drooped a little now, she was thinner than ever, her hair and teeth of a similar hue. But so sweet, with shapes.

The following morning, he took an extra *Metro* and made the Carsons his last stop, though hesitant at the doorbell. 24 Oak Road. The doorbell chime sounded like a dog barking, presumably Paulie's idea. He hoped Susan would answer.

She did, surprised to see him. She was wearing blue today.

'Wilf. Are you okay?'

'Do you want a *Metro*?' he said, then, 'I'll bring it every day.'

'Oh, Wilf,' said Susan and, to his surprise she came down off the doorstep and put her arms around him, hugging him like his mum used to, only a lot smaller. She lay her head right on his chest and snuggled it.

'That's so nice of you. We'd love the *Metro*.'

At this point, Paulie appeared behind her, his two-tone face peering from the hall.

'Worzel', he said, 'are you a Jehovah's Witness now?'

'Paulie, stop it. Wilf's come to visit.'

'Good. About time. Don can take a running jump.'

'Is Don here?' said Wilf, alarmed.

'No. The fit-to-live stuff.'

'Ignore him, Wilf,' said Susan. 'Please, come in.'

'Have a beer,' said Paulie.

'I don't drink beer.'

'Vodka.'

'Tea,' said Susan.

Wilf felt torn. A step inside was a step in the practice of conversation. But his soul literally dragged him back as if with fingers clasping his collar. In the end, he couldn't do it.

It wasn't Susan, it was Paulie, who still had an aura. And discomfiting, pearl-like eyes with no lashes or brows.

'I don't drink tea,' he lied.

'Well, let's have the paper, then,' said Paulie, taking the *Metro*. 'Do you read it yourself?'

'Stop, Paulie,' said Susan, giving him a dig. 'That's their joke, Wilf, you can deliver the paper but can't read it. That's the level they're at.'

'I can read.'

'Bet you read more than him,' said Susan. 'I think my brother . . . Have you anything to say, Paulie?'

Paulie stared – he seemed to have lost the ability to blink. Wilf grew aware that if skin is burnt it takes patience to learn how to re-use certain muscles underneath.

'Sorry, Wilf. I won't call you Worzel anymore.'

'Not to your face, anyway,' clarified Susan.

'No, I mean it,' said Paulie.

'Woo-hoo,' said Susan. She gave a little clap and winked at Wilf.

'Are you two always like this?' he asked.

The twins laughed at the same time.

'When we're together,' said Susan.

'Was that a joke?' asked Paulie. 'You can rehearse a few new ones for down the pub.'

'Don't even think of bringing him to a pub.'

Wilf looked from one to the other.

'Good day to you,' he said and walked away.

'See you tomorrow, Wilf,' called Susan.

As he walked, Wilf felt something new. He'd rung a doorbell and made recruits. It banished his lingering headache. He felt Paulie wasn't disgusted by him after all.

Later, when he spoke about the visit to Felicia, she confirmed Big Don was spreading a verdict that Wilf wasn't fit to live alone anymore.

'Ignore him,' she added. 'Don't listen to anything about a petition. It's sour grapes. Don't tell or think.'

Wilf didn't understand the references. So, decided to follow her advice.

29

HIS fox. It was evading him.

The rascal troubled his thoughts. He'd only seen it once. He wanted to see it again.

Ensconced in a hole in the cemetery, it reverted to nocturnal habits. It emerged in moonlight with its vigilante gait to gobble up food, and nowadays that wasn't a long or stressful search. Wilf would never see it again unless he lured it into his view.

He scrabbled in his memory to retrieve what he knew about foxes. Details felt distant and close.

His mum had a moulting fox-fur wrap, inherited from a grandmother, one of her few things left from Ireland. She'd thrown it away one season, on a tidying spree. That day she'd cleared out a scaly kettle, a small sculpture of Discobolus that chipped when Wilf bumped it to the floor, and a copy of a book called Malachi's Cove he was reading. But the fox-fur stuck most in his mind. His mum could hook the fox's teeth into its tail to pin around her shoulders. It had marbly glass eyes. It seemed alive.

He felt a longing to feel the texture of its fur again.

He remembered that foxes breed in winter. Cubs are born in March and have a life expectancy of three years. By his reckoning, his pet must be about seventeen months old. Its mind was probably obsessed by mating, although it might already be a father.

Looming in his thoughts was a certainty he could see it again only at night.

Night was a word that brought a special dread to his mind, like "police" or "handcuffs".

He decided to wipe it out of his thoughts, for now. He was afraid of the dark outdoors.

30

SUSAN Carson went for a few drinks with Aoife O'Dwyer, Felicia's daughter, who was around the same age.

'By the way,' she said, 'tell your mum Wilf called round.'

'Fucking trainwreck on your doorstep,' said Aoife, who was devoted to swearing, because it always pissed off her mother.

'Wilf is *lovely*. He is, isn't he? Isn't he, Aoife?'
'Ah, he's alright. But he takes up too much of Ma's time.'
'Oh, did I tell you,' added Susan, 'Norris is getting parole?'
'Are you looking forward to seeing him?'
'*Mmmmm* . . .' said Susan, almost purring.

That same evening, Wilf was getting bogged down by Oscar Wilde. He came across a word he didn't understand. Every time he opened the book, he remembered the word, and the pages seemed to close again.

Wilf didn't know exactly how he understood so many words. It was a lifetime's saturation of newspapers, school texts and his mum's rotational reading routine, the intensity it forced. In many ways, he'd read more than anyone on Yew Road, except Professor Emma.

And she was the obvious solution. Wilf realised it with relief. As soon as he understood this word, he could read normally again. He would ask the Professor, living in Number 50, who knew everything.

He went out to do so, almost with a bounce in his step. But, when he got to her door, new nerves came. He reached out, almost turned away, but ultimately rang her doorbell.

He heard the soft purr of Professor Emma approaching. She opened her door with a winding dexterity.

'Wilf. Are you okay?'
'What does intracrural mean?'
'No idea. What's the context?'
'Intracrural.'
'I heard that, but do you have any . . . clues?'
'Men.'
'Men?' Professor Emma smiled as if recollecting good times. 'I suppose that narrows it down by about 50%. I have a bright idea. Why don't I give you a dictionary? Know how to use one?'
'Alphabet.'
'Just so. I'm going to choose one. I own a lot. But I'm keeping the Chambers '44.'

Professor Emma drove backwards and to her left, while Wilf

waited, listening. There were short, almost imperceptible spurts of engine sound.

She arrived back at the door with a large, bright book on her lap.

'Encarta. It's a bit flash but well researched. It's got pictures. It's too heavy for me, I don't like handling it.'

Wilf took the dictionary, which filled both of his hands.

'You don't have to read all of it,' said Professor Emma. 'But it helps.'

What she said made sense. She had a clear mind.

He turned away in a hurry, but stopped, remembering something. He turned back and said, 'Thanks.'

31

WILF remembered something strange about fox cubs.

When they're born, they can't thermoregulate. The heat in their bodies is out of sync. They're hot and cold.

Mother Fox cosies up. Her fur surrounds the cubs. But with freezing earth beneath, they must keep twisting and turning and roiling to get free of cold bits, or hot bits on another side, writhing against brothers and sisters. To a fox, it must seem like a second birth struggle.

Then one day they stand on their own four feet. And thermoregulate.

They learnt survival.

Stranger still, as he thought about cubs squirming, he felt what "intracrural" meant. It was intense physical friction, proximity, comfort and discomfort. He sensed rather than defined it. Which was good because the word was not in Encarta.

Professor Emma had chosen the wrong dictionary. But to his joy he could read Oscar Wilde again.

32

AFTER his success with the Carsons, he thought hard about whose door to knock on next. But his old, familiar dread was still clinging.

So, he drifted back to consoling routines. He walked the streets. Delivered *Metros* to safe places.

One morning, he saw all three Toms come out at the same time. It was hilarious. When they realised their error, Bulfast Tom flung a glare right, English Tom a sneer left, and Mayo Tom, in the middle, slammed his door.

He saw Beardy Callum buy a bottle of Carta Roja wine in Spar, wearing his most diaphanous black frock. He saw Island Garth, whose wife kept him well-away from money, stare through the huge window of the Masons Arms pub, watching Manchester United play a football match on a big screen TV inside. Eventually, someone in there might grow guilty and beckon him in for a drink.

When Garth was young, he was an outstanding guitarist. He jammed with Bob Marley in Soho and Notting Hill. Garth could twang out rhythms like a juggler. His wife, exasperated by endless noise, cut all his guitar strings one night, so he didn't play anymore. But practised with his fingers on the stringless fretboard.

On another morning, Wilf found a £10 note in his hallway. The crackpot poet must have passed his door. Days were good.

He met Ray who wrote for the *Times*, bringing home groceries. Ray stopped politely, as he sometimes did, and offered a handshake.

'I'm sorry I don't have any change, Wilf. I wanted to give you something, but I'll do it tomorrow.'

Luca the Frenchman caught up with him while he walked along Beech Road.

'Wilf. I found this in the street,' he said, holding out a £20 note. 'I think you dropped it.'

'No, I didn't,' said Wilf.

'Well, take it anyway.'

Any more of this, and Wilf thought he would be rich.

33

AND suddenly he *knew* he was changing.

The world was all pain and no tranquilisers. But his interior life was getting better. He was slowly, gradually for the first real time eroding the dread that had surrounded him all his life. All his activity was making him stronger.

He was losing his dread of people walking towards him on the street, his dread of eyes making sideways glances, his annoyance at people saying, 'Are you okay?'

He even said, 'Hrymmphh,' in a lighter tone.

He lost his biggest fear of all . . . Ana, the Czech woman. She was the scariest person he knew because she worked for the police.

Usually, when he saw her, he shrank inside himself. She was tall, spare-of-speech, decisive. She had authority.

Felicia, after Ana's party where she danced in fishnet stockings, told him a secret about Ana, which normally prompted Wilf to feel less scared of a person. But the bizarre thing was, he lost his fear of Ana *before* being told.

It happened on a routine, while he was tired.

He always shopped hard after Torture Tuesdays, in the supermarket on the Grove. He'd haul bags of food home, hanging like anchors from his hands. He bought a lot, because his most irregular routine was money. If he had it, he needed to spend it, because, if he needed it, he never had it. Money eloped with private companies.

He shopped unpredictably. He loved the brief power to buy.

He bought fruit and boxes of cornflakes and tea lights. He liked hard pears, that no longer grew on his mum's tree. He never bought

Flake bars, which he felt were his mum's love gifts rather than a standalone foodstuff.

He bought more than usual that day.

Ana, by coincidence, was walking towards him on Yew Road as he went home. She had her way of scrutinising you as you approached. She observed his four supermarket bags.

'I'll carry the heavy one,' she said, taking one of them. She did a U-turn and walked beside him to his house. She was utterly silent.

At his gate, she handed him his bag, said, 'Goodbye,' and strode off.

As he watched her body, he thought the way she held herself was like an alluring, moving painting. He understood why someone wanted to marry her.

He repeated this later to Felicia, who then told him Ana's little secret.

Ana had been a police cadet in Prague but had to drop out because of money. She took a bus to London and found a job in Pizza Express. She studied and studied in her spare time and took police exams and, though her English was often incorrect, passed ahead of everyone else. Ana was now a Metropolitan Police Officer.

Her first assignment, with a fellow fresh-qualified cop, from Poland, was to dress as a prostitute.

They – Ana and Elle – were posted on streets in Hackney, waiting for drivers to stop. The ones who did felt relaxed to hear women talk in an East European accent. After agreeing business and a price, Ana or Elle would gesture to an unmarked car that drove over to pen in the offender.

Elle issued a lot of police cautions, but Ana issued more. She wore a catsuit.

Now she was taking exams to be a detective. So was Elle. A firm friend.

It was why Ana chose Whores & Clerics as her engagement party theme. Felicia said all the vicars were pay grades below her.

Elle was there that night too. She wore a tight dress starting mid-breast and ending mid-buttock. It was no longer work clothes.

34

OUT of the blue, one Monday, Eileeen with three 'e's asked for a *Metro*.

'Willlf,' she rasped in Texan, as he walked by her house. 'Stop or what?'

He stopped and looked back. It was a bright evening. Eileen was leaning out of an upstairs window, eyes bluely bobbling on him. She lived in 8 Oak Road. He hadn't known that.

'I thought you might, could bring me the *Metro*. Is it a big deal?'

Wilf found he couldn't say anything.

'I mean, would it be a problem?'

'No,' he said finally.

He spread his hands to show he had no newspapers.

'From tomorrow. Do you drink coffee?'

Wilf hesitated.

'I mean, percolated, the real thing?'

'I drink tea and coffee.'

'Come on inside. You don't have to talk. I talk all the time.'

Eileen was also keeping a secret. Felicia had told him. In real life, she wasn't a gardener. She was a lawyer on a string of losing cases, close to losing her job.

'But I promise I'll stay quiet,' she said, withdrawing from the window.

He stood still, waiting near her door. After a while, she opened it. She swung back silently into her home, leaving it wide open.

He edged in and looked around. It was like walking into Professor Emma's den, but different. He closed the door and stared about.

It was open plan, but no stair lift. A bookcase held books, but with empty spaces. On the floor were all types of obstacles, a cheese plant, a sculpture that grew into tentacles, a sofa with cushions, a coffee table where Eileen had dropped a Vogue with her mobile phone on it. He was transfixed by a print of The Dance, hanging crooked on a wall. He'd seen it before in the book by Phaidon. It was a Matisse painting. Its colours were intense. Hanging crooked made it better. He felt Matisse would agree.

'Over here, hunk,' said Eileen.

She was waiting in the kitchen unit. She had placed a colourful bag on the counter. She also had a small machine on the other side.

She pointed at each in turn.

'These are Cuban coffee beans. This is a grinder. I'll twist off the top and show you how it works.'

She twisted it off. Wilf watched her pour cleft brown beans onto its screw. When it was full, she tightened the lid and pressed it down. Loud scrunching sounds erupted and she fought with the twitching machine. Finally, she took off the lid and showed him a fine brown powder.

'It takes time,' she explained.

She now unscrewed the lid of a small grooved-bellied coffee pot and tamped the powder in with her fingers. She lit the gas and put the pot on the flame.

'Now, watch this,' she said.

She pointed at a transparent knob on top of the pot lid. It was made of a sort of crystal or glass, with a thin tube in its centre. Wilf watched.

As the water in the kettle heated, a drop spat at the top of the tube, and trickled. Then drops bubbled up, then steam obscured them.

'It's how Americans make coffee,' said Eileen. 'Have you seen it before?'

'I don't live in America,' said Wilf.

35

EILEEN kept her promise. She stayed quiet. She poured him coffee in a small cup. He asked for milk.

'Try it black.'

He did.

He nodded, though it tasted sour and hot.

He looked over at The Dance. Then wondered how to get out.

Eileen seemed to have anticipated this too.

'Thanks for stopping,' she said, slapping his shoulder like a man, 'don't forget my *Metro*.'

He tried not to rush to the door. But as he did, he had a sudden thought and turned back.

'The iris,' he said.

'The iris?'

'It doesn't need watering.'

'Why not?'

'It'll grow anyway.'

'Ah, I get it,' said Eileen. 'Never lose sleep over a flower.'

Wilf nodded and left in a hurry, relieved that pregnancy hadn't been brought up again. His nerves felt light, as if swimming.

He strode to the end of Oak Road, then headed straight up Ash Road all the way to Chamberlayne. He slowed down, almost to a crawl, as he passed and studied the oranges outside the Italian café. He felt drawn to the life in the way they lay. They were like a Matisse painting. The café was about to close.

He turned around and walked the blocks back home.

36

JUST as other people had secrets, Wilf had paintings. They were his secret. He absolutely loved paintings, especially real ones, in oils.

As a child, then as a youth, his mum took him on many day trips. Quietly, so as not to disturb others, she explained things they saw, to try to focus his attention on the realer world. He was her different little boy, but she was determined he grew into an adult who could express himself and be independent.

She brought him to London Zoo. To the Victoria and Albert Museum. Kew Gardens. Hampstead Heath, where boys flew kites. The Natural History Museum. The National Gallery. There she noticed his instant attraction to art. She brought him to other galleries like the Tate and Hayward. The little boy would look around in wonder until finally, he would fixate on a single painting, and stare at it until his mum tugged him away.

It was the same at the Zoo. He would choose an enclosure, and focus, and forget the other animals.

At home, he was able to describe paintings down to the slightest detail, and describe animals as clearly as in a documentary.

She brought him to the Everyman Cinema, twice, to see the same film, Crocodile Dundee. She brought him to the theatre, twice, to see the same play, Peter Pan, where one of the actors had big ears. But afterwards, she finally accepted he'd never truly absorb human synergies in two or three dimensions, and was mostly elsewhere, though he said, after the cinema, 'They shot kangaroos.'

She brought him to poetry readings, but he dozed off to the drone of self-absorbed voices.

She brought him to a concert by the London Symphony Orchestra. But he panicked at the sudden clash of Beethoven and had to be pulled out within minutes. She never risked him with opera.

Of it all, it was art he remembered most vividly.

Since her death, he rarely left the vicinity of the tree streets, the cemetery, and the supermarket on the Grove. But he read in an *Evening Standard* dated October 8th, 2006, that a big gallery, the Saatchi, had opened in Chelsea. He wished he could see that.

It had new paintings.

37

HE dreamed about his mum again. An intense, cryptic dream. The two willow trees had divorced and swung in opposite ways. His mum sprang from the ground in her favourite pink blouse. Oscar Wilde's mum, Speranza, left her grave to pay a visit with her high bosom and swinging Victorian ringlets. Wilf's mum, tsking, sat her down and loosened the ringlets, shaking out her hair into a fiery red cascade.

They set up a chess board on a table and played. It didn't surprise him. His mum often played chess with herself, until one day she saw a chip on a bishop's shoulder and decided to throw out the set. It was around the time she stopped seeing the Vicar of St. Aubert.

Speranza and his mum made fast competitive moves. Their pieces flew, until they forced each other to a stalemate. Then they sat, hands on chins over the board. Slyly, both reached into bags at their feet. Each drew out a glass and a bottle. Each passed their glass to the other, then poured from their bottle into the other's glass. They toasted. His mum made a sudden chess move and rapped the table.

'Checkmate.'

When he woke up and thought about the dream, Wilf decided this was a clear signal – make a new move. It must be to do with one of his two concerns. Finding more *Metro* recruits or facing up to night, where his fox roamed.

38

WHEN he went out to feed the pigeons, Felicia came out of her house.

'Wilf,' she said. 'Eileen phoned me last night. She'd still like you to help with her community garden.'

'No.'

'Why not? You don't have anything better to do, and you might like it.'

'It's the Council's responsibility,' said Wilf stubbornly.

'The only thing Brent Council's good at is evading responsibility,' said Felicia, turning away in a resigned frustration.

Wilf took an extra *Metro* on his round. He knew a house where he might find another recruit. 17 Beech Road. Make a new move.

But it was a high-risk house, in the sense that it was home to a perpetual rotisserie of tenants. It was among several in the tree streets rented out cheaply by a private landlord. It had been turned into sub-rooms occupied by foreign men, sharing a bathroom.

But one was Irish, so different.

In Wilf's mind Irish people weren't foreign but born misplaced. Ideally, the neighbouring island should be an uninhabited wistful land, Britain's holiday layby. His mum was from Waterford, as was the Irishman in Number 17, who had the word Waterford tattooed on his arm above three yellow boats on a blue shield.

His name was ... Wilf didn't remember, but thought it may be Oisin or Oscar, like half of his book. He seemed like a good prospect because Wilf had once seen a copy of the *Irish Post* newspaper sticking out of his back pocket.

The problem was that Supine Mario also lived in Number 17 and he was obviously foreign. Wilf often imagined Mario struggling up off his bench at nights to get to Beech Road, finding his way home and opening his door, collapsing onto a narrow mattress in a tiny room, having snorted, swigged, spliffed for an eternity of hours, finally home, collapsing, in some way distinctly different from a Brit collapsing. He hit his head when he fell sometimes, getting cuts and bruises.

When he got to Number 17, Wilf found that the knocker had broken off its door and the bell had lost its pushing nipple. This gave him pause for anxiety, but he finally lifted his fist and rapped with his knuckles.

He prayed the Irishman would answer. In his mind he rearranged phrases he'd thought of and settled on, 'I brought a *Metro*. It's free.'

His skin crawled as he heard voices, and coughs as someone approached.

The door was opened by Supine Mario, who tilted out almost to the 10-degree angle of Wilf's gatepost, but like his gatepost, failed to fall.

Mario lips swarmed into a smile.

'Wilfie, my man.'

Wilf's skin crawled again. Something was not right with Mario's face. It looked like he'd caught a disease. Patches of his cheeks and nose had pinged out zits of differing hues, pink towards mauve. He might have snorted an allergen. Wilf leaned away.

Mario opened his door wide, tilting almost 10-degrees back, and swept a hand to the interior, 'Come-c'mon. Breakfast.'

Wilf abruptly turned and walked away, dropping the *Metro* to the ground.

'Wilfie,' said Mario, plaintively, ''s'okay, don't go.'

Something disturbed Wilf deeply about that face, and sent his thoughts into a whirl. He made long strides to the end of Beech Road in step with long breaths, as his mum once taught him, guiding him to stride up and down the hall of their home as a boy, to teach him restraint if she'd observed anger filtering into him. He brought calm into himself and started to reason it out.

Mario's new face was no worse than Paulie Carson's. Paulie was burnt by a gas explosion from the outside, Mario seemed to burn from inside. They both took drugs and drank. But Mario was foreign, there was a difference. He leaned closer. Wilf remembered a poem by Auden, saying that British people have "*pagus*", a unique personal space. If someone entered it, it made them feel like spitting. That explained his resentment towards Supine Mario.

He felt this way because he had *pagus*. He was British. It was his fault. Was this the aspect of him Felicia didn't like?

She entered his mind with her big direct voice, speaking out against injustice. Racism was her pet hate.

'The only good racist is in a minority of one,' she said.

Wilf was always in a minority of one.

But Mario didn't have a race, he was just foreign. Felicia spoke out for them too. As if a race.

He decided never to think about Number 17 and its inhabitants again.

Plus, it was obvious. The door-to-door routine had to stop. It was too distressing.

He realised he was standing on Oak Road. Mothers with children on the way to the infant school were eyeing him.

'Beetlejuice,' a kid called.

39

NEXT day, Wilf had a dull headache as he delivered *Metros*. He put a copy through the vertical mailbox of Eileen's door.

He was walking away when he heard her rasp, 'Willlf. Stop or what?'

He turned to where she leaned out of an upstairs window.

'Have you heard the news? I won a case.'

'Did you take your nose ring out first?' he asked.

'How'd you know?'

He didn't know what to reply. After waiting a few seconds, she gave him a wide grin and swung shut the window.

It confirmed what he now knew. He already had enough crackpot *Metro* readers to keep his hands full.

40

BEARDY Callum boarded a bus with Felicia as they went to Harlesden to shop for cheap fish, cheeses, wine and household products. Nobody sold meat cheaper than Jim Lyon, but for most other bargains tree street residents went to Harlesden.

People liked Callum a lot and had gotten so used to his dresses that it was sometimes a surprise to see him in men's clothes, as he was today.

They talked about Wilf.

'You know,' said Callum. 'I've always thought of writing a story about him. His mother and all that, how she tried so hard.'

'With photos?'

'Aye. Do you think Wilf would like reading about himself? Maybe I can get it into the *Metro*.'

'Oh my God,' said Felicia, 'he'd shit himself.'

But Wilf was already 'shitting' himself at the thought of going out after dark. It was the next new move.

His mum had rarely taken him out any evening since Beethoven. After that, she went out alone and gave Felicia a few quid to come over to stay with him.

For some reason, his mind associated going out after dark with her loss, as though whatever killed her had been caught out there, at night.

But his fox was out there.

Finally, the simplest of ideas came to him.

Why not take a routine from day and switch it to night? After leaving food for his fox, he could take a walk, just like his pattern in daylight.

He felt a cargo lift from his shoulders. Night was simply another routine.

He remembered in his bedroom was an alarm clock, found on one of his walks. It was buried under a pile of clutter. It took him a while to find. It was an old mechanical, with a big fascia and two bells rung by a little hammer. It had an inset dial for setting the time for the bells to ring. He decided to set it for midnight judging the hour now from light on the wall. Then, he wound up the clock.

The big minute hand twitched. He waited but the mechanism was frozen. He gave the clock a shake. Nothing happened.

He remembered something Felicia once said, over ten years ago. Big Don had a job then as a driver. His truck stalled one evening on Yew Road, as he drove it back to the depot. Don climbed heavily out of the cabin with a lump hammer, opened the truck hood and struck the engine hard. When he resumed his seat, the truck started perfectly.

'Brute strength and pig ignorance work sometimes,' remarked Felicia.

Inspired, Wilf threw his clock hard against a pile of newspapers. It bounced to the floor without breaking. When he stood it upright on the table, it started keeping time perfectly.

But that night, he slept right through the alarm. He woke in the morning with a headache.

He felt he'd let down his fox. It missed a feeding. It had possibly been forced to spend the night scavenging rubbish.

He set the alarm again and, on the second night, it woke him.

He'd left a tea light burning at the top of the stairs, casting glows and shadows. He descended, with some kidneys in a clipping from his scarf. When he opened the door, streetlights pricked his eyes. The sky was unfamiliarly eerie and vaultlike. Despite a sudden panic, he forced himself out and shut the door behind him.

More slowly than in day, he picked his way down Yew Road. Nobody was about. The roadsides were jammed with parked cars. At the corner by the ball court, a pungent smell drifted into his nostrils.

He recognised it. Skunk, the onerous weed Supine Mario smoked.

Two dealers were seated on the bench, talking. He saw blips of light as tokes were taken. He wasn't afraid of them. Weed made people groggy. They would sit adrift, till a car drew up and fingers with money protruded. Drug dealing was a dull job.

He rushed across the road with his head down and went through the little gate into the playground. At its far side was a clump of bushes. He trotted over and pushed his gift under the leaves.

He thought of waiting a while, sitting on the parents' bench. But then felt, no . . . he needed to complete the routine.

So, he walked. He took the long stretch of Ash Road to Chamberlayne, then ducked back into the tree streets and walked up Spruce to Beech and to the intersection with Yew. He saw a few solo pedestrians, and a late crowd was thinning in the forecourt of the Corgi Inn. But the streets were otherwise deserted.

At home, he shut the door firmly and made his way to bed in tea light. His mission was accomplished. He'd overcome his fear of the dark outdoors.

41

THE next morning it rained hard. Summer thunder skedaddled, loud but roving. His broken gutter delivered dollops of water on weeds growing in his back yard.

Rain never deterred him from his daily rounds.

He pulled on an anorak found in a bag of clothes on a street. But as he walked to the station, he decided to take advantage of something rain always deterred – parents and children.

He went into the empty playground and headed to the bushes. Pushing back branches, he saw the meat was gone, a blue patch of his scarf left bloodied and shaken away.

Pleased, he carried on with his *Metro* deliveries. He got home soaked to the skin, but rain was also a prompt to change his clothes. To him, washing and changing were too erratic to be routines. Washing meant cold water, since he had no heat, and changing was just a nuisance delayed until he felt clammy.

Now, he changed all his clothes. His next routine was to take another walk and he wanted to get out. But rain was persistent, grew heavier. It splattered and as he looked through his window, he saw flood water in the gutter backing up from a blocked drain outside Number 22. He decided not to go out again.

Instead, he sat by a window with Oscar Wilde.

He chose page 123 at random and read about Oscar's new home at 34 Tite Street, Chelsea, adorned with designs. The Wilde family were visited by Prince Edward, who shared dinner with Oscar, making witty conversation. When Wilf paused, phrases in the passage fused in his mind, and he seemed to hear the Prince joke, 'Not to know Tite Street is not to be known.'

A fresh idea dawned on him, congealing around that name, Tite Street.

Tite Street was in Chelsea, and so was the Saatchi Gallery. Why not make visiting them, as well as other places, a new routine? Just go.

It would take some planning. It was his most ambitious change yet.

42

HE carried on next day as normal. As he was walking past the ball court, he saw the three gardeners working again. The smaller one, Marcus, stood up and raised his smartphone to record Wilf.

'Hey hey hey,' said Eileen, 'Wilf doesn't like being filmed.'

'Oh, sorry,' said Marcus. 'I just thought it was a good visual. Maybe make a tree streets video diary.'

'Not with Wilf in it.'

'Then it wouldn't tell the full story,' argued Marcus. 'London neighbourhood, warts and all.'

Wilf was trying to hurry past, but the wiry one, Oliver, strode out in front of him with his hand raised for a handshake. Wilf shook it.

'We haven't really been introduced. Oliver Sewell. I'm sorry you can't help us with the garden. Your iris is just the right type of plant.'

'Watch out for that one, Wilf,' said Eileen. 'He's a Christian QPR supporter. Hates Arsenal and abortion.'

'Who doesn't?' said Oliver. 'Do you have a church, Wilf?'

'St. Aubert.'

'The one near the Grove? That's Church of England, isn't it? I'm a Catholic.'

'So was my mum,' said Wilf.

'How come you're different?'

'I'm always different,' said Wilf, turning and rushing back the way he came.

As he was walking along Ash Road, he heard his name being shouted. Looking back, he saw Big Don sprint forward. Don was still roaming the streets after his mother's death, and recently was carrying a clipboard and knocking on doors.

'Wilf, wait, I want to talk to you.'

Wilf ran. Or rather, through habit, walked fast. Big Don was also run-walking, huffing, but Wilf had far more practice. He outpaced the big man easily and fled to Yew Road.

Once home, he panicked and took long paces and deep breaths from his hall door to his kitchen and back, and back again. He felt cornered.

Now, he *had* to go to the Saatchi. Just to get away. The tree streets were turning into an obstacle course.

43

BUT that night, at last, he saw his fox.

Climbing to his room in daylight, he set the alarm again for midnight. Then he lay on his bed and tried to sleep, though it was bright and the trauma of the day was still in his thoughts. A breeze outside that rustled the leaves of his mum's old pear tree lulled him slowly to sleep.

The clock woke him with hammer and bells. He got up.

Still sleepy, he wound a strip of scarf around a lamb bone saturated with flesh and went again to the children's playground. He placed it in the bushes near the corner.

This time, he sat on the parent's bench and waited, crossing his legs.

Light traffic breezed on the Harrow Road to his left. He heard a few voices on the Green opposite the backpackers' hostel. Backpackers came out there to smoke.

The smokers drifted off and the traffic lightened more. The breeze had fallen. The beech trees behind the cemetery wall seemed pinned in place.

He sat a long time, hours, seeing nothing. Cold seeped into his body, even though it was so summery.

He felt it was a failed night.

But just as he was about to go home when he saw a shape. It moved fast enough to be unidentifiable.

Wilf waited, as still as he could. Nothing happened. He was breathing slowly, watching carefully.

Then it was there. A fox in the playground. It trotted straight across his vision to the corner bush and, waving its snout in a brief navigational sniff, plunged right in.

Wilf saw it backing out, with the bone in its mouth, shaking its head because of the scarf. The fox turned and looked directly at him.

It was his big dog fox.

The one from the thicket. No one could forget its ears, pointing.

Abruptly the fox lopped fast towards the Harrow Road, taking its dinner home.

44

ELATED Wilf felt pillars of success soaring. Inhibitory ones tumbling. Everything lifted his spirits again.

It was all coming together. By now, he was delivering more *Metros* and had doubled his book count (he didn't see *The Birds* as a book, but as a mother-object he had not been given permission to read).

He said 'Hrymmphh' less often and he'd seen his fox. A wonderful animal.

He was changing himself. In his own way, at his own pace.

The next day he went through his *Metro* round and other routines feeling carefree. Even when kids started lifting their phones as he passed the playground, calling him 'Smelly Kelly' to get his attention, he didn't look at them or feel threatened.

The image of his fox, its resolution and fearlessness, caused his mind to think more firmly about when to go to the Saatchi Gallery. He'd do it tomorrow.

He'd go to Chelsea tomorrow morning.

So that evening, he prepared. He thought of what to wear, wondering if he wore a muted jacket and pair of old blue jeans, he might pass as inconspicuous? Improbable, but he realised maybe for the first time in his life he felt a need to consider what other people thought of him.

He thought about how to get there.

His mum took him on day trips in three ways. By car, if heading out of town or to Hampstead Heath. By Tube, if going to central London. At points as a boy, they stopped at every station on the line except Elephant & Castle where, his mum said cryptically, you could find no elephants, castles, or hope.

Most of all he liked the third way, walking. She liked walking too, on Hampstead Heath, or in Regent's Park, where he trailed her on paths and cross-paths, looking at other things. A few times, she walked with him all the way to the Thames, through Kensington and Chelsea. They stared at the rat-coloured river together.

On their way home, they'd seen a clump of old soldiers, Chelsea pensioners, seated outside the Royal Hospital, in their scarlet uniforms and tricorne hats. To him, they were like a painting.

He'd walk to Chelsea. Just as he used to do with his mum.

45

So, next morning, he set out.

He knew it was a long way so put a few sausages in his pocket. He filled a plastic bottle with water from the tap.

The easiest part of his walk was the stretch to the Grove. After that he had to push himself to continue. He never went this far anymore.

After a while, it grew less scary. He recognised things. The shops behind the pillars in Notting Hill Gate were still there. The restaurant with the marlin over its door, where his mum stopped, and read the menu prices up and down, then sadly gestured him on. They'd sat outside the Churchill Arms a few yards further, where she bought ham sandwiches, with mustard packages.

He walked through the Kensington back streets. He remembered seeing those tall red-brick buildings.

On busy Cromwell Road, with its museums, he stopped. He walked to the nearest traffic lights and waited for green.

Soon he found himself in the atmosphere of Chelsea. It was like the tree streets, but without apparent neighbours. It had narrow streets of distance, congestion without community.

Oscar Wilde had lived in these empty streets. Wilf remembered that, in his era, people socialising on streets were servants. Outdoors was working class. Indoors, you designed drawing rooms, to draw your own class. His mum once said, 'The rich don't need property, they need to avoid common yokes like us.'

This was Chelsea, a place where people like Oscar avoided people like him.

He recognised the King's Road and crossed it.

On the other side were the final blocks to the Thames. He walked until he saw the corner he remembered. It was a three-block street with a pale blue nameplate saying, Tite Street.

He'd noticed it back when walking to the Thames with his mum. 'Not to know Tite Street is not to be known.'

Not far down, one of the row houses had a spheroidal plaque on its front. He drew up to it, Number 34, and read, 'London County Council OSCAR WILDE 1854–1900 wit and dramatist lived here'.

He looked at the windows. Net curtains. Oscar lived behind nets. Speranza had walked up those four steps to visit her son. Did she have a key or ring the bell?

He had an impulse to put his hands on the door, he didn't know why.

But he turned away.

A few streets over lay the Saatchi Gallery, his real destination.

His mum had once pointed to a beautiful building on one of their walks. 'Know what that yoke's called?' she asked. 'The Duke of York's Headquarters. Who's he when he's at home?'

Obviously of no importance since the building was now the Saatchi.

As he drew near, he felt anxiety. What if there was an entry charge? He hadn't thought of trying to find out. He felt he should stop, U-turn, but pressed ahead determinedly.

When he got to it, no one bothered him. People barely looked at him. No security guards. A rope barrier prevented him from going upstairs, so he wandered around the ground-floor galleries.

They held a bewilderment of choices. The spaces were a dazzle. The white fir floorboards seemed to lead straight to each painting. He turned in a circle in the centre of each space before walking into the next.

In the final space were fewer paintings and no installations. The sign by the door read, 'Samples'. The room held works by new artists who 'sampled', 'riffed' or 'improvised' on masterpieces. The sample and the masterpiece hung side by side.

Wilf saw a painting from a distance.

He went right up to it, staring hard.

It was beguiling, a buff-brown force.

It showed a woman on her side. She seemed a distillation of every woman he'd ever known. Bits of all were in her, his mum, Felicia, Emma, Eileen, Ana, Susan Carson. She lay in resignation on a bed in front of a man, who stared elsewhere.

The man resembled him, the way he looked at other things. Except that in the painting he wore glasses.

A card said the woman's name was, 'Patricia Preece'. It was one of the masterpieces, on loan from the Fitzwilliam Museum in Cambridge.

He stared at it a long time. He didn't notice the sample beside it. His mind didn't work that way.

When he finished staring, he went home, munching sausages while walking.

46

'HAS Wilf ever had an IQ test?' asked Eileen, sharing another bottle of wine with Felicia. She had set out Texan delicacies: buffalo wings, jalapeño 'poppers', guacamole and tortillas.

'No, why do you ask?'

'He was staring at one of my prints, that Matisse over there, like he knew something about it.'

'Wilf knows a *lot* more than you'd ever expect.'

'Thought we might, could get him, I dunno, a test. Maybe find some specialist, like, therapy for gifted matures.'

'Stick to men your own age, Eileen,' said Felicia.

'Y'all kidding?'

'Wilf wouldn't agree to it anyway.'

Felicia tried one of the poppers and pulled a face.

'Tastes like one of Wilf's socks,' she said.

Two blocks away, Wilf was thinking about his fox, while Felicia poured more wine.

He longed to entice it to his home and reasoned out his next tactic. With his mum's scissors, he cut thin strips from his scarf.

Late at night, he left his house with some pork cubes and the strips. The pork didn't smell at all and, in fact, the meat he got from Jim seemed fresher than before. Maybe Jim suspected he was a secret cooker?

He left a cube of meat randomly in the playground, with a scarf clipping.

Then at the corner by the ball court, he dropped another piece of meat. Then walked a few yards further and dropped a piece of scarf.

In this way he left an alternating trail of meat and scarf along Yew Road. When he got to his house, he left a final piece of scarf at the gate.

The glass panels on Wilf's front door had been smashed years ago. Someone had thrown stones through them, while he'd been under arrest and sitting in a police cell. Felicia's son, Vince, had screwed corrugated iron over it but, being a sloppy worker, left a gap. A space for draughts but, also, a spy vent, for looking out.

He applied his eye to the vent and waited for his fox.

He waited hours, switching eyes regularly as each dried out.

Nothing happened. He thought he saw a shadow at one point, then it was gone.

Finally, he emerged. Walking back along Yew Road, he saw all the scarf pieces, but the meat had disappeared.

He knew his tactics had worked. He could repeat them.

Pleased with himself, he went for a late-night prowl.

47

It was a beautiful night. Fragrances were turning autumnal. The streets were cosy with fragments of the day's warmth. A few lights were on in houses, where night hawks were surfing the net, writing books, or drinking themselves to early graves.

He was walking alongside Mr and Mrs Gupta's tall garden wall on Ash Road (they were on their annual holiday in Gujarat), thinking it could provide excellent support for overhanging honeysuckle vines. Suddenly, he heard sounds on the other side of the bricks.

He stopped and stayed silent.

A foot in sneakers appeared on top of the wall. Then a man hauled his body up, resting briefly at the summit. He wore a backpack and was trying to move as stealthily as possible. Finally, he swung into the street and turned to find himself face to face with Wilf, who recognised him instantly.

'Norris. You're out.'

Norris, ashen faced, dark eyed and bleach haired, stared at him, jolted. Then he went on the attack. He forced Wilf roughly against the wall, with his elbow pressing his throat.

'Worzel,' he hissed. 'I'll cut you. Shut it.'

Wilf tried to breathe.

'Shut.' Norris finally released the pressure.

Wilf stood stock still, as if pinned like a butterfly on a page.

'Hrymmphh,' he said finally.

'Shut that too. I hate it.'

Wilf was frozen. Norris grabbed his face and rammed his head back against the wall.

'Say nothing. Got it?'

And then it was over. Norris ran light-footed to the corner and swerved around, backpack joggling in expert silence. Wilf took long breaths and found himself pushing his shoulders hard into the wall as if it might swallow him. When he gathered himself together, he saw he'd torn a sleeve.

Norris was gone.

Wilf rushed home, terrified.

48

WHEN he got indoors, he sweated profusely. He sat on a chair and his head lolled. Shaking, he got up again and found his way upstairs. His tea lights had gone out, so he stumbled by memory. He fell onto his bed and was asleep instantly.

He had a terrifying dream.

In it, he walked on Birch Road and, on its bench, Big Don and Norris sat. They ran at him. He froze. Behind them, hundreds of children came hurtling. They pressed close, like boys in a crescent at school. Their faces no longer had eyes. Instead, there were crows' heads in every socket, cawing. Desperately, he looked for help. He saw his mum and Speranza in the ball court. They were tossing a frisbee to each other. Between them his fox leapt joyfully, trying to catch it. They couldn't see him. He was beyond help.

He woke next morning with a splitting pain in one side of his head. He had a high tolerance threshold, but this was above, like catching his finger in a door inside his brain.

After shambling a while over cornflakes, he decided to do something out of the ordinary – see Felicia. But when he went to the front door, fear flooded in. He breathed hard, gripped the lock bravely, and yanked the door open.

Sunshine made his eyes blink.

He crossed straight over to the house opposite and gave his usual four rings on the bell. Felicia answered with a hungover air, but a look of concern crossed her face.

'What happened to you, Wilf?'

'I have a headache. Do you have tablets?'

She studied him closely.

'You look shit. I'm taking you to a doctor. Right now.'

'I'm fine.'

'No, now. You said you had a headache. Don't contradict yourself. I'll get my bag and we'll go to the Charles clinic.'

'I'm not going anywhere,' he said, loudly.

'Wilf.'

'No.'

'Okay, no drama,' said Felicia, backing down. 'Hold on. I'll get some co-codamol.'

She turned inside, without inviting him in. Nobody would have known she was furious, but Wilf knew. He felt his normal intuitions coming back. Felicia had tried one of her wiles, but it hadn't worked.

She came back with a blister strip of tablets and instructed him not to take more than two, and not to finish the strip today, but keep some for tomorrow if his headache was still there.

As soon as he got home, he swallowed four with water. Then stood in the kitchen, wondering what to do. His day was ruined. There was no point in picking up where he left off. His pigeons would have to feed themselves.

He sat at the table, to rest before his *Metro* round. He wondered how he would be able to go out again at night but knew he had to.

After a while, the pain receded, then faded into nothing, and his head was clear. He felt his thinking come back to normal, though a little different.

He regretted going to Felicia. It would raise her curiosity and questions. It was vital he gave her no clues about his fox. She'd intervene, even though it was her who told him to get a pet.

His mum taught him about wiles – trifling with one's better or worse nature. It was one of her old 1960s beliefs.

'Wiles are to women what guns are to men, Wilf,' she said, 'weapons of war.'

Felicia used three of the normal five – the mother, the sister, the daughter. She was mostly his sister.

But at the door she'd tried her mother wile. If she'd used the daughter wile, and pretended she felt ill too, and could he help her to the Charles please-please, he might have relented.

The final wiles were the grandmother and good-time girl, but he'd never met any of his grandmothers and couldn't remember many good times, especially with girls.

49

FELICIA was waiting next morning when he went out to feed the birds. He hadn't taken any more tablets, but before he could offer back the remainder, she folded her arms in front of him.

'Well, what was all that about?'

'I had a headache.'

'Come on, Wilf. What happened?'

'I had a headache.'

'Okay, be like that,' she said, and walked off shaking her head. She knew him. She shouldn't push it right now.

He knew her too. She would swing back to it.

He realised with dismay he was growing apart from her. A secret, his, now lay like thin muslin between them.

He went through his daytime routines, including (since the date was the 13th) sweeping out his kitchen floor and pushing the dirt far out into his mum's garden. It seemed to be appreciated by weeds, which grew into its successive layers silently.

He was feeling much better. His skull was free of pain, his pulse and breathing were normal, and he was clear-minded.

He went to bed in daylight and set his alarm again for midnight. He planned to repeat his fox trail as before. But this time, he'd draw the animal to his front door.

When he woke, he put food in his pockets and left the house. To his surprise, he didn't feel the least twinge of fear.

He went to the playground, but stopped, and now *did* feel fear. A man was sitting on one of the children's swings. His instant thought was: Norris.

But as his eyes adjusted, he saw it wasn't. It was the poet from Number 3.

His first instinct was to turn home. He restrained himself. He watched the poet twitch the swing back and down with his heels, his arms draping round the chains, head down. He was the last on the *Metro* round who Wilf still felt shy of. Suddenly he decided it was time to change that. He surged forward, letting words emerge.

'Is it your second childhood?

'No, whiskey.'

Wilf noticed a bottle in the poet's hand. He seemed unfazed that Wilf had materialised abruptly in the dead of night.

'Is it because of your poem? Are you still stuck?'

'Poem?'

'About the dead girl in the cemetery.'

'Oh, that? No, I finished it. It's called, The Leaning Stele of Tessa. Do you want to hear it?'

'No thanks,' said Wilf.

'I'm having a bad night,' droned the poet. 'I drank galore and stormed out of my own flat after a fight with myself in an empty room.'

'Rooms always win.'

'Shout out, bud. Thing is, I wrote a book. I thought I was dead, my creativity. I thought it was dying. But no. I wrote a book while I was asleep. Called Glass. I wrote drafts, struck out words, invented characters, and began with the sentence: 'I read this in Tolstoy and wept because it was so true.' I've never read Tolstoy. The plot led me on a search. But no matter how hard I tried to find out what I was looking for, I met invisible barriers. The "glass" of the title. But in the end, I got it.

'My final draft was magnificent. I mean, beyond the Booker, beyond the Pulitzer, Nobel stuff. Then I woke up. I wrote a classic but can't find a publisher.'

One hundred per cent crackpot, thought Wilf.

'Irish writers, eh? My name's Kevin Curran, by the way.'

'I know. Felicia says you're wanted by the police'.

'No, I'm watched by the police.'

'What did you do?'

'I think it's they want to know what I am doing.'

'Are you a terrorist?'

'Do I terrify you?'

Wilf thought about it for a few moments.

'No.'

'There's your answer.'

Wilf said nothing. He looked at the silhouette of beech trees swaying above the cemetery wall. He watched a night bus rip past on the Harrow Road. Then he nodded, before walking away.

A thought made him turn back again.

'I read Tolstoy War and Peace,' he said.

'Are you winding me up?'

'The woman ends up with the bookworm with glasses.'

'Shout out, Wilf. But you gave away the ending, I can't read it now.'

As he walked home, Wilf realised he had just held a normal conversation. About literature.

50

AT home, he waited an hour. Then went out again.

The playground with its skeletal children's climbing frames, swings and slide, was isolated. Kevin Curran was gone.

Again, he left an alternating trail of meat and scarf. He ended it by leaving a small cube of lamb a foot inside his gate and a piece of scarf on his doorstep. He took up vigil at his spy vent and waited.

Hours seemed to pass. His eyes felt cold and dry, and he switched from one to the other.

His fox appeared, abruptly, coming straight inside the gate. A quick sniff and it gulped the food. Then it stood, indecisive, its ears primed. It looked at Wilf's door. He felt it sensed him. It lolloped away.

Then it came back, still indecisive, its forepaws twitching. It came towards his door and almost disappeared from view, apart from its brushy tail. He could hear its snuffles against the jamb.

Then it walked back out and stood on the pavement, alert.

As softly as he could, Wilf opened the door.

He had hardly widened it a crack when the fox ran away.

51

ISLAND Garth was standing in line at Spar when Felicia joined the queue for the cash register.

'Mi see mi man Wilf,' he said. 'He up to something.'

'Why do you say that?'

'He have a big shit-eating grin on his face when he deliver the *Metro* this morning.'

'I bet I know what happened,' said Felicia. 'I bet someone put some money through his door again.'

'Can they put any through mine?' asked Garth.

Wilf was indeed walking around with a private smile and new confidence. He was trying not to feel excited. Trying to carry on.

He tried to talk to more people. Tried not to feel besotted by a fox.

He was less afraid now of not knowing what to say. Kevin had made him realise that people talked for their own reasons. They made it up as they went along. He'd never seen it that way before. He'd always felt people had an underlying hostility. But they weren't all like Norris or Big Don Jones.

On Wednesday, coming out of Spar, he came across Beardy Callum. Callum was sitting outside the Spanish café, in a neat blue dress with jeans underneath. Wilf noticed the dress had darker blue trimming from the shoulders converging to the chest, artlike. Instead of walking by, he stalled, swaying.

'Are you okay, Wilf?' Callum asked, in his Scottish burr, from somewhere Highland or Lowland.

'I'm fine.'

'Do you want a coffee? It's *café con ron*.'

'What's that?'

'Coffee with rum. There's never a reason to drink *café sin ron*.'

'What's that?'

'Coffee, naked and alarmed.'

'What language is it?'

'Spanish. I learnt it in Cuba. I interviewed Fidel Castro.'

'In a dress?'

'No, I wore a suit. I worked for Marxism Today. It's defunct now. But its best-ever issue was the one with my Castro interview and an essay by Eric Hobsbawm.'

'Were you a journalist?'

'I still am.'

'Which papers?'

'They blacklist me, mainly. Can you not tell from the way I've ended up?'

'Ray writes for the *Times*.'

'Ray Houghton? Keep the heid. I rate him. He writes for the extortionist media, but about walks in the country. They're observant.'

'Ray's nice.'

'I know. And you're not so bad. Are you going to have that coffee now?'

Wilf thought of the rum, and said, 'No'.

'No worries. Remember, keep your mind awake and your desire asleep. It's what keeps you, you.'

Wilf had no idea what that meant, apart from too much rum. He was walking away, when he had a thought, and turned back.

'What did he say?' he asked, then remembered to add, 'Castro?'

'He said there's never a reason to drink *café sin ron*.'

'Is that all?'

'He talked a lot. But if you want a précis, I'd say, he thought capitalism is in control for now but needs Cuba's coffee, and that would rot its foundations. He was wrong. But it felt more diplomatic than inciting a global revolution.'

Wilf didn't know what that meant either. He still remembered the sour taste of Eileen's coffee. He went home.

Then, he remembered. It was Wednesday. He had forgotten to buy his chips. He hoped the Portuguese woman wouldn't feel offended.

52

TALKING to Callum was like watching his fox move in mysterious ways. Callum was a big old dog fox, his beard like a ruffle.

He thought of Ray Houghton. If anyone understood foxes, it was Ray.

Ray was quiet, balding, short, with a strange coat that looked like it was made from mouse fur. He'd once been starvingly poor.

As a child, his father was in and out of work, his mother drank, he ate dry bread and had holes in his socks. They moved around till they ended up on Yew Road. When he left school, Ray found a job as a lavatory cleaner on Chamberlayne Road. In his spare time, he wrote articles about his walks in the cemetery and Regent's Park and mailed them to newspapers. One day in the silly season, August, when nothing happens, a bored editor read one of these handwritten articles.

He wrote a letter back, asking Ray to write more, and offering to send a typewriter. There was a cheque enclosed. Ray used it to open a bank account.

He became a stalwart of the *Times*. Every fortnight, he sent something new, and even wrote a novel, which sold moderately and reached a paperback distribution of 14,000 copies. When the Council offered his parents the opportunity to buy their house at a discount, he raised a mortgage.

He got rail fare now, and hotel allowance, to visit faraway gardens and trails. He avoided Scotland. It was too far except by plane, and he told editors he didn't like flying, thistles, or bagpipes.

He had a slight spinal curvature forcing a slight stoop. It made him almost as withdrawn as Wilf, which was maybe why he so often slipped him some money, as if they were in a conspiracy of misfits.

Wilf read some of his columns about nature walks. They were filled with detail, such as how blackberries seemed to change digitally as they ripened, turning green to red to black pip by pip, until all black, but you still had to wait, and feel them lightly to see if they were soft. If they were soft, they were sweet.

Wilf often thought of that as he passed the blackberry bushes in the cemetery. In the silly season, in August, he reached his long arm through their thorns, cupping his fingers on berries, testing for soft ones. He loved their taste, though seeds got stuck between his teeth.

Ray wrote about rabbits, foxgloves, oaks, stag beetles, adders, slugs, and a family of foxes he watched colonising an abandoned greenhouse.

Wilf briefly longed to see him almost as much as he longed for his fox, but didn't meet him on the streets. It never occurred to him to knock on Ray's door.

53

WILF concentrated on his fox. He didn't feed it for a few days. He wanted it hungry enough to compromise on its instincts, to risk coming closer to him, to be seduced.

He'd use the same tactic that brought it to his door. He believed he'd have to repeat it again and again, feeding by feeding.

He set his alarm for later than usual, two a.m.

He put on an extra jumper in case it got cold and made his scarf comfortable beneath his trousers.

He woke up before his alarm went off. He deactivated it but waited for the clock to reach two. before leaving. He watched it by tea light.

Outside, from the playground to his house, he dropped a few, very few, slivers of meat.

Just inside his gate, he put a fat sausage on the ground. He reasoned that if he couldn't resist Jim Lyon's pork-and-leek sausages, what chance had a fox?

He sat with his back against his door and set down more sausages between his feet.

He was prepared for a long vigil, but in less than twenty minutes, glimpsed a flash of fur between parked cars. On the road.

He waited.

His fox appeared, walking more slowly than ever before. Once it locked eyes with him, its gaze didn't waver. Wilf lowered his eyes submissively.

The animal began to slink forward, intensely alert. Suddenly, deftly, its muzzle darted sideways in the gate and whipped up the sausage.

It ran away.

Wilf lifted another sausage in the air, dangling from his fingers, and put the final sausages behind his back. He waited.

The fox returned, again slowly. It stood at the gate, indecisive. Its forepaws twitched as he'd seen before.

Wilf did what he always did, but more patiently than usual. He looked elsewhere. He kept perfectly still.

From the periphery of his eye, he saw the fox move slowly. He waited.

Then he felt, as if by persuasion, the sausage guided from his fingers. When he moved his head back, the fox had gone.

It never returned.

But his pet now knew if it needed food, it would have to eat from his hand.

His fingers tingled. He almost felt breath on their tips.

54

FROM the window of the house opposite, Vince O'Dwyer, Felicia's son, had noticed Wilf sitting on the doorstep, while he finished a late-night joint. He watched him for a few moments. He saw that Wilf was staring at a sausage and had more between his feet.

'Fuck, Worzel's getting madder,' he thought. He was glad his sister was asleep, otherwise she'd Instagram it.

As he turned to get back into bed, he decided not to say anything to his mother. Felicia was up to her eyeballs in other worries, not least Big Don and that stupid petition.

But in the morning, as he ate beans on toast with the family, he couldn't resist a small remark to Felicia.

'Hey, Ma, do you think Wilf might really not be fit to live alone?'
'Yes, he fucking is,' said Felicia, swearing in front of her grandkids.
Vince decided to keep his mouth shut after that.

Wilf, meanwhile, knew his fox would return. It had accepted his human lair. But only ate two sausages and a few strands of meat.

It would be hungry and expectant.

The next night, he went out again. This time, he left no food in the street. Instead, he dropped pieces of scarf in a trail, returned and sat outside his door, with sausages between his feet.

He waited.

The silence was broken by two cats fighting, their yowls jarring clearly over roofs. A quiet car, a Prius, slid silently over the speed bumps, running on battery. The driver was a stranger.

He waited.

Nothing happened.

After a long while he felt a mild shiver and knew it was time to stop. He entered his house and walked sadly back into his kitchen, where tea lights burned.

He thought about Oscar Wilde and thought about sleep.

Suddenly, he heard a bark in his back garden. An abnormal 'Hrymmphh' bark, in the unique banshee frequency of foxes.

He opened his back door and there, in the wavering candlelight, saw his fox.

It sniffed the air, energetic and eager, turning, looking, sniffing, trotting, returning, its eyes on Wilf.

He meekly took the sausages from his pocket and lay them outside the door. They were gone in an instant. The fox disappeared into the weeds.

He sat down heavily on his chair. A sense of bewilderment came over him. How had it got into the garden? The back gardens were enclosed by terraced blocks. He swayed back and forth.

Through a vacant house. A few were always being renovated. Some waiting for new doors or windows. A fox could find a way.

He couldn't see it. But it was near, really, really near.

After a while, he turned to Oscar Wilde, knowing he wouldn't sleep. He pulled around pages and found a photo of Oscar kneeling over a severed head in a stage play. He didn't like it, so randomly opened page 119 where he read about Speranza.

He read for hours, at peace in the knowledge his pet was safe.

55

WHEN he finally slept, he had another dream. He was in a restaurant lush with paintings and hanging plants. The waiter, who happened to be Norris, approached with a platter and, whipping off the lid, presented him with his fox's head, a sausage in its snout.

It woke him up. He hated that dream. But knew what it meant. He had to keep his pet in absolute secrecy.

He carried on with his routines. As expected, Felicia found a way to swing back to his headache.

She'd coaxed him into her house, for a shower. After it, he sat in Vince's bathrobe, eating stew. She looked at him calmly over the kitchen table.

'Tell me what really happened.'

Wilf was prepared.

'I fell,' he lied. 'Dark. Hurt my head.'

'You were up in the dark?'

'Cup of water. Fell. Hurt my head.'

Felicia sighed at him with a newer, milder stoic look.

'Getting old, Wilf. Clumsy.'

She reached across and squeezed his wrist. She was ageing too. She shifted her shoulder in the air, as if trying to soothe an aching clavicle. She'd seemed harried lately. He'd seen her on the streets, knocking on doors.

'But you're telling lies.'

Wilf said nothing.

'Someone hurt you, didn't they?'

'No,' said Wilf.

'Okay. That's good. That's good.'

She watched him eat stew.

'Anyway, you don't need to worry about Big Don. He only raised ten signatures for the petition and I've spoken to nine. They've withdrawn.'

'Who'll he send it to?'

'Social services.'

'Should send it to the Council.'

'They don't own your house, love. You do. They can't put you out, they can't put you away, nobody can do anything to you.'

'Owners always win.'

'Don did it to get at me. He wants to hurt me through you.'

Wilf didn't know what she meant but sensed it was serious.

He plunged his fork through a baby potato in his stew. He felt its tines pierce a piece of chicken beneath, so could lift vegetable and meat to his mouth at the same time.

'I like the taste of thyme,' he said.

56

'HEY, Ma,' said Vince a few days later, still unable to get over the thought of Wilf on his doorstep, 'does Wilf like sausages?'

'You know he does,' said Felicia. 'I cook them for him. Why?'

'Ah . . . hhh, no reason. I thought I saw a sausage sticking out of his pocket.'

'That wouldn't surprise me,' said Felicia.

Wilf was focused heavily on sausages and other foods as his life began to take on a new pattern.

In the evenings, he prepped food by cutting meat into strips – ribbons of liver, pork belly, loops of tripe. After dark, he sat on the back doorstep, and dangled a morsel. At first, his fox wouldn't come, and his arm tired. It was only when he sat sideways, with his face averted, that he heard a rustle and felt food being guided away.

Over nights the animal grew less shy. One night Wilf left his back door open and lay mince on a newspaper page in his kitchen. He sat reading Wilde by candlelight, turning pages slowly. And slowly also his fox, pausing at the door, slipped into the kitchen, grabbed a mouthful of food and retreated.

Night by night, the fox progressively lost its wariness, came in with a soft trot, and fed from Wilf's hand as he sat, reading, studiously avoiding eye contact. He left his back door open all the time now.

He felt a sense of wholeness and trust. He decided his fox must be highly intelligent. A stupid one might have taken over a year to tame.

In quiet hours, he thought about life and routines. He felt a need to review everything, understand, hold each thing in front of his mind to judge its worth. Even his most sacred routines.

On walks in the cemetery now, he liked to imagine that his fox was trotting beside him like a dog. He wondered if at some point he could make that happen. People might accept and admire him as a unique man who'd tamed and trained a wild urban fox.

One day, he found himself near the Celtic cross where first he'd followed his fox. He paused, squinting at its curlicued carvings. He decided to go closer and trod warily over the rough ground.

Its base held a long, long inscription. He read:

'Requiescat Jane Francesca Lady Wilde, née Elgee 'Speranza' of 'the Nation' writer, translator, poet, nationalist, early advocate of equality for women, author of works on Irish folklore wife of Sir William Wilde, mother of William Oscar and Isola, born Dublin 27 December 1821, died London 3 February 1896.'

It was Oscar Wilde's mum, for real.

He turned his head in a direction, thinking. He knew where his mum's grave was. Not far. Should he visit her? Could he finally accept that she was dead?

He stood, wondering whether to go. To stand over her grave.

57

THERE were some routines he knew he would always, always cling to.

His *Metro* round was too precious.

St. Aubert was too warming. He still went there every Friday, for hot food.

He had two guaranteed hot meals a week, Felicia and St. Aubert, and a third every fortnight, chips from the Portuguese woman.

St. Aubert was a long walk, as far as the Grove, but he always felt secure as he approached the big shoulders of religion. He never went into the church itself, through the lych-gate, but instead rang the bell of the vicarage.

The Vicar set aside his biggest room every Friday to feed the needy. He kept it empty except for chairs and tables to eat at. He drew in a microcosm of the London underclass – the old and cold, hungover, refugees, the toothless and swollen-jointed, homeless junkies, and Wilf.

When it got full, the Vicar went out and tied rosary beads on his gate. New needy knew to turn away when they saw that.

Though not a Catholic, he liked beads and was a chirpy cleric. He was a High Church aficionado who'd once been a hippy and, now in his seventies, kept his ponytail. He always listened to what the Pope said in Rome as closely as to the Archbishop of Canterbury, his boss in England.

Wilf was one of a select few allowed to arrive early and claim a place. His table was sometimes the last to fill, as the needy streamed in. Then came soup, poured by the Vicar and his wife from flasks, meat-and-two-veg, and sweetness in a bowl with custard. Everyone got a baguette as they left.

Most ate quietly. Some didn't speak English.

The Vicar always wove around and found time to talk to everybody. He had smile-lines on his eyes and sometimes held long exchanges. Occasionally, he succeeded in wooing a new spirit to his Sunday Service.

As the room emptied today, he sat in a chair by Wilf who sipped his custard. He was patient. They'd known each other a long time.

'So,' he said finally, 'what do you think about God this week?'

'Hates angels. The flapping makes his eyes dry.' Wilf was thinking of the eye vent in his front door.

'Was that one of your mum's ideas?'

'No.'

'Ahh. But it's good. I like it. It's true, why can't God get grumpy? If man is made in his image, then vice versa, has to be grumpy sometimes.'

'We're better off without him. My mum said that.'

'I know. She told me every time I saw her.'

The Vicar crossed his legs, in a leisurely way.

'Now, don't get offended if I say this, Wilf. You've changed.'

Wilf didn't respond.

'I mean, you're less edgy. You don't jerk and twitch as much, like you want to walk away all the time.'

'I like people,' said Wilf, out of the blue.

After a while, as his surprise and pleasure subdued, the Vicar said: 'I suppose people take a long time to get used to. I mean, actually, it's amazing.'

'I try to talk now.'

The Vicar said patiently, 'In my work, Wilf, I meet good, sad, and angry people. If I meet someone evil, I almost thank God. Otherwise, it's boring. But it's someone – incommunicable – that's the hardest.'

'Don't give back.'

'. . . Yes,' said the Vicar. 'That's exactly what I mean.'

Wilf said nothing.

The Vicar knew him well, so lifted himself up lightly, and tilted his head in respect. Wilf wanted to be left alone now.

As he walked home, he realised he'd always liked the Vicar.

58

MAUREEN Gonne was running the washing machine when her husband, Mayo Tom, came into the kitchen.

'Do you think Wilf might like these, for the winter?' he asked, holding up his old pair of Foxford mittens.

'They'd be too small for him now, Tom. He's a big fella.'

'No, wool stretches. It shrinks if you wash it but stretches if you wear it.'

'Well, you try to persuade him to put those on, and see how far you get. He'll think they're baby gloves.'

'I'm not that small,' countered Tom. 'I'm taller than my brother.'

Wilf, oblivious to his neighbours' good intentions, carried on living his new life, in peace. He thought deeply about himself, and about his past.

He fished through his youngest memories for rediscoveries.

His mum took him out so many times as a child and talked about where they were and what they were doing. She repeated Tube station names as they left trains, stopped and pointed things out. She asked questions to ground him in detail.

'Where are we now, Wilf?'

'Walm Lane.'

'Number?'

'36. Shops. Eazy-Dri Kleeners.'

He understood those questions now, fed drip by drip, as if he were a fox and questions were fox food. They were to make him more aware of where he was and what was happening around him. She'd sometimes stop him as he came in from school.

'What day is it, Wilf?'

'Thursday.'

'What did you learn? Wilf . . . look at me. What did you learn at school today, love?

'Cos.'

'What's Cos? Is it lettuce? Is it an island?'

'Cosine,' said Wilf. 'Adjacent over hypotenuse.'

His mum gave him a hug.

'You're a clever yoke, you are.'

He understood her now in a way he was unaware of then.

Now he was a man, a reader, a homeowner, a pet keeper. He learnt many new words from his Encarta. Mikvah, a cleansing. Metempsychosis, a rebirth.

He felt like he was in a second birth struggle.

His fox was more relaxed and would rest just outside his kitchen door, watching. If Wilf grew absorbed in his book, it would find a way to get attention, coming in, snuffling. Then he would feed it a morsel. It was otherwise a respectful pet, and never soiled inside. Not only was it more natural with him, he felt natural too.

He only now realised how thick its tail was, and how it held the tip down or up, down, down, a bit up, straight and went on alert, if Wilf made a movement too fast. He would have liked to lay a hand on its back, while running his other along the brushy moss of fur.

Like a brush of his own, he still wore the scarf in his trousers. Shorter, it seemed a part of him now. At times he imagined it was a Scotsman's sporran. But he knew he should throw it out, the way his mum threw used stuff out.

He wondered if he should throw out Oscar Wilde when he finished reading it. Thinking it over, he thought, yes. He'd toss Oscar into the bin.

Professor Emma was giving away boxes of books. He thought of asking her for a box, but it was too much. He would ask for a single book when finished with Oscar, and would choose it himself.

Mostly, he thought of visiting galleries. He longed to go again to the National Gallery, in Trafalgar Square. But even for him, it was a walk too far.

To get there, he'd have to take a Tube train.

That would mean facing up to more fears, of crowds.

59

'How's Wilf doing these days,' Professor Emma asked Felicia, who had dropped by her house to borrow a book. Bulfast Tom was there too, fixing a blocked sink.

'Oh, he never really changes,' said Felicia. 'I thought he was coming out of his shell a bit more, for a few days. He called round to Susan Carson.'

'And took two books from me,' said Emma.

'I knew a man like Wilf in Port of Santos,' said Tom, working with a plunger. 'Went round trawlers begging for fish, then went round slums handing them out.'

'That sounds more like St. Francis of Assisi,' said Emma.

'Yeah, but did Francis leave his flies wide open with no kacks on?'

'Wilf never did that,' snapped Felicia. 'Don't even go there.'

'Well, at least he's reliable with the *Metro*,' said Tom.

Wilf still collected *Metros* early to deliver. A few mornings later, he was outside the train station, waiting for the delivery van. He was thinking about the National Gallery.

It was still dark and the station gates were locked. Floral scents from the Green offset a fumy smell from the rail lines. Minutes seemed to drag. Dark lingered but he felt air and sky lightening.

He abruptly remembered that a house on Beech Road was being renovated. Outside it was a skip with debris and tossed-away stuff. He'd given up hoarding but thought it might be interesting to see if anything new had turned up. People threw all sorts of things away if they saw a skip on the street.

So, he took time out to stroll to Beech Road.

As he neared Luca the Frenchman's house, he noticed its front door was open. When he got to Luca's gate, he stopped, jolted.

Luca was lying on his front path. His fingers were twitching and eyes blinking. Blood spread around him, seeping from his throat. As Wilf drew near, Luca's eyes seemed to lock on him.

Wilf didn't know what to do, then abruptly did.

He dipped his hand into his trousers and tugged out his Foxford scarf. It was still long enough to fold a few times around Luca's neck, and Wilf delicately lifted the injured man's head as he did so. He pulled it gently tight, and pressed his thumb firmly over the bleeding wound, as his mum taught him to do whenever he cut himself.

Luca looked at him with mild, rational eyes.

Wilf said nothing but waited, keeping steady pressure on the wound.

Luca blinked at him more slowly. His eyes and face were gentle.

Wilf sensed him slowing, slowing, fingers falling still. Finally, there was a long pause after he blinked. Then the slowest blink. His eyes fixed on Wilf again, but no more blinks came.

Luca the Frenchman was dead. His nostrils seemed to widen slightly.

Wilf's strength drained and slowly he stood up. He didn't know what to do. He felt confusion and a type of guilt, like at his mum's death. But Luca's tranquillity calmed him and drifted him towards thinking more clearly.

He remembered his *Metro* round.

He rushed home. His hands were bloody, and he'd wiped them on his clothes by reflex. Any newspapers he touched would be destroyed.

He shoved into his house, not even thinking of his fox which still got spooked by sudden movements. Luckily, it was nowhere to be seen.

He raced upstairs to the bathroom and held his hands under tap water. He rubbed them together and watched a diluted rosy swill twirl down the plughole. He stood a long time, hunched over, rubbing his hands.

Finally, he stopped, allowing them to dry naturally in the air. Then he went to his bedroom and changed all his clothes, pulling on a jacket that Felicia bought him recently. He noticed his shoes were still bloody, so used the vest he had taken off to clean them.

He sat for a while on the side of his bed, breathing slowly.

After a while he went downstairs and drank a cup of water. He looked out into his back garden, where his pear tree writhed in the sky.

Eventually he went to deliver the *Metro*, with one paper less.

60

HE was more agitated than he'd ever been in his life. At one point, he ran abruptly at a squirrel, sending it scurrying in panic up a tree.

He didn't even linger outside the three Toms. He imagined Luca still lying on the ground, unnoticed.

When he got home from his deliveries, he found a £20 note in his hallway. Kevin Curran must have passed by outside.

He sat at his table with the money, staring for a long time into the eyes of Queen Elizabeth II. As he stared, the Queen's smile seemed to grow mysterious, like the Mona Lisa's.

Then an idea came to him.

He could go to the National Gallery.

He'd made no decision on when to visit it. He was broke. But now he held the train fare in his hand.

Without thinking more, he stood up and walked straight out, around the corner of Yew Road towards the station.

Inside it, the clerk, behind her barrier of glass, refused to sell him a ticket.

'You have to use the ticket machines,' she explained, pointing.

He turned and stood at a hulking machine, with a line of instruction: TOUCH SCREEN FOR TICKETS.

He stood a long time. Finally, he realised the clerk had come out of her enclosure and was standing beside him.

'Where do you want to go, pet?'

'National Gallery.'

'You need Charing Cross station. Return?'

He nodded.

'Best option is a one-day travelcard. Got money?'

Wilf handed over his £20 note. She made taps on the screen and fed it into a slot, which sucked it greedily from her hand.

A ticket and coins were spat out as change.

'Put it in the slot at the barriers,' she said. 'Okay, pet?'

Wilf followed the instruction, and the barriers opened. He went down the stairs to a platform. A digital screen overhead said, ELEPHANT & CASTLE 3 MINS. He waited.

A train hurtled in purposefully, like a parakeet headed to roost. He got aboard and sat down.

As it shook to speed, he looked around at other people. The carriage was half full. Everyone minded their own business.

But their business bothered him. All – some with earpieces – were absorbed in phones. Staring, listening, tapping the screen, scrolling their fingers up and down, down and up.

No one was reading a book or newspaper.

They were so heavy, so sad looking.

He found himself shuddering. They had to pay for phones. Books could be found on streets or garden walls, thrown away.

Metros were free.

The train stopped at stations. People got on and off, some brushing against his trousers. He hated it.

He felt his agitation mounting.

The wheels screeched as they curved into Paddington Station. When the doors opened streams of people flooded onto the train with luggage: backpackers, tourists, from Heathrow Airport.

In a panic he stood and pushed against the crowd. He got off just as the doors closed behind him. He felt the whooshing draught of the train depart.

On the other side of the concourse was the platform that could take him home. He went to it immediately.

It seemed, on the journey back, he was floating above himself.

As soon as he left the station, he walked up Oak Road and turned on to Beech Road.

Further along, he saw a police car with a flashing light. Blue ribbons had been tied across the street, and uniformed officers spoke to each other.

61

AFTER seeing that, he spent the rest of his day as if hypnotised. At home, hunched over, Luca in his mind, he sat hours on a sofa between newspaper heaps in the front room, watching light change through a tear in the curtain. Cars, footsteps, voices passed outside, filtering in as if amplified.

It was dark when he went back into his kitchen, and ate cornflakes with his fingers from a box. He'd eaten only cornflakes today. The back door was open and nothing stirred outside. He sat down, lonely.

A longing for companionship came to him.

'Hrymmphh,' he said aloud, in a tone he remembered from before.

A few moments later his fox appeared at the doorway, peering with a tilt of the head, twitching its forepaws as if making its mind up. Then it came inside, sniffing and alert to his movements. As it settled on the floor with head on paws, Wilf realised it wasn't hungry. It was waiting until it got hungry, and in the meantime had chosen to lounge as if among family.

Wilf began speaking to it.

He didn't think about what he was saying. He focused on his tone, even, calm, a whisper. He kept it steady. He never looked directly at his pet. He said what words and thoughts came, and after a while the image of Luca faded, and he began to feel better.

He found some meat to leave his fox, then rose in darkness for bed. While he slept, he had another dream. In it, Speranza met again with his disinterred mum. They climbed over the cemetery wall and sat by the canal. Taking off their shoes, they dangled their feet in the water. They chatted about their sons and his mum said, 'Sometimes with Wilf, he showed a little glimmer, and I knew he was listening.' 'Oh, Oscar never listened,' replied Speranza, 'he had far too much to say.'

When he woke the next morning, he felt back in a good place. He was thinking clearly again and decided to carry on with his daily routines. He thought about trying for the National Gallery again.

But before he did his *Metro* round, he brought the papers home and read one. He wanted to find out if there was a report on Luca.

As usual, his eye got distracted by other stories. He found exactly the type of news item he loved, about a family man who went on a drinking binge. A few mornings later, stumbling home, the man ran into a large group led by the police, headed for the forest. Finding out they were searching for a missing person, he joined in. After a while, amid trees and ferns, he heard someone shout his name. He replied, only to discover he'd been searching for himself.

Wilf laughed at this.

But then he saw a news item on page seven.

MILLIONAIRE FRENCH RECLUSE MURDERED

He read that Luca Vignal, a French expat, had been found brutally murdered. The bachelor, who moved to London in the 1990s, lived unknown in a modest house in Kensal Green, despite drawing substantial income from property holdings in Paris. The family of the millionaire owned a resort near St. Tropez. Police were investigating the possibility of a hate crime linked to Brexit.

Wilf closed the paper.

It was true. Luca the Frenchman had a secret.

62

HE felt a sense of panic grow inside him.

He'd let Luca down. He should have rung Felicia's door as soon as he'd found him. But he hadn't thought of it.

An old form of fury welled, like when he was a boy and got angry whenever his mum stopped him doing things, stopped him from being himself, insisting, 'no'. He'd stretch out sometimes and sweep something to the floor.

She'd stare at him, tilting her head down.

'May your memory last longer than your temper,' she'd say. 'Are you my blessing or are you my curse, child? Think, Wilf, think.'

And as Wilf thought about that question, he really couldn't say. But it grounded him and he forgot why he was angry.

He felt fury subside now and realised Luca's death wasn't his fault. It made him grieve. He could grieve for the French foreigner, like he'd grieved for his mum.

Then an idea came to him and suddenly hope began to return.

After the *Metro* round, he'd try again for the National Gallery. He didn't have to go through this welter of emotions.

63

So, this time, he prepared better. Before leaving, he ate a pear and a packet of crisps. He filled up a plastic bottle with tap water.

At the train station, he remembered how to use the machine, dropping the coins of the previous day's change into a slot.

During the Tube ride, he used a tactic. He hunched himself up and didn't look at people. After a while, he grew more comfortable with their proximity and the way each ignored each but saw all with motions of their eyes.

By Piccadilly Circus he was sitting up straight, and at Charing Cross almost skipped off the train in anticipation.

But he nearly didn't make it to the National Gallery. The platform walls at Charing Cross were lined with reproductions from it, including the cartoon of the Madonna and Child, by da Vinci. He'd seen it as a teen, with his mum. It was an image of rhapsodic beauty. He stared at it alone for long instants.

But he was able to tear himself away.

He followed tunnels and went up stairs, until he found himself on Trafalgar Square. The winner of the Battle of Trafalgar, Nelson, stood high in the air, on a pillar. On the far side of the square was the Gallery with its Greek columns and portico.

He walked, weaving around tourists. Pigeons landing to peck had to skip and fly out of the way of human feet. Wilf stopped to watch.

Did the energy they got from pecking equal the energy of getting out of the way?

He almost stayed to watch longer.

But the National Gallery was right there. With all sorts of sculptures outside.

As he got closer, he realised he wasn't looking at real sculptures, but at crackpots wearing costumes and body paint, pretending to be statues. They left boxes and hats on the ground where passersby could drop money. Maybe they were an art installation? He thought installations might be better suited to the Saatchi. He felt like clasping the legs of a silver man standing in the air and pulling him to the ground.

Ultimately, he ignored all of them.

Inside the Gallery, after he'd gone up many steps, he was free to see whatever he wanted to look at. Wilf walked around the big spaces, circling sometimes. He felt he had to find something that spoke to him.

Then he stalled at a painting. He walked close to it, then stepped back, to give art its *pagus*. It was called *Bathers at Asnières*, by an artist whose name sounded zoological, like *sewer rat*.

It was a painting of a hot day by a river in a place where private companies had built factories whose high chimneys smoked in the background. A few males and a dog the colour of a fox rested on the riverbank. A boat was on the river. Two boys were bathing. One was big and bold with a red hat, hollering to someone on the far bank. The second was an almost invisible boy, his back turned, hunching over, vague as if elsewhere.

It was him. He was that boy.

Wilf discovered he'd been searching for himself.

64

OVER the next days, he kept largely to himself.

He thought about who he was, what type of person. 'Contumacious', his mum said. Though he knew its meaning, he confirmed it in Encarta. Stubbornly defiant to authority. 'Contumacious slinger,' she'd say in her old-time Waterford slang if he ambled too slowly behind her.

Other people called him retarded, in the third person, as if not seeing him standing close enough to touch.

He was neither of those. He was a brooder who liked to brood deeply by himself. He liked to put his head down and turn away. People's voices so often sounded like radio interference.

He felt he was an actual man now. Britain was home to seventy million people. If he could focus on being one in a million, it meant there would be sixty-nine others like him across the island. He'd no longer be a minority of one.

He even wondered if he could get a job, to pay for light and heat? That might be the next challenge, the next routine.

What type of job might suit him?

Night watchman at London Zoo or at a gallery? Making sure all was calm and, if it wasn't, pressing an alarm button. Maybe walking around and stopping to look at the leopard and ocelot, who woke up at night. He might prefer the Zoo.

He asked himself if Andrew Shaw, his Work Coach at Jobcentre Plus, could find him a job there. Improbable. Andrew would just squirm his eyebrow in embarrassment, before saying there were unlikely to be vacancies at London Zoo, and experience with wild animals was a requirement. Andrew might not be convinced that experience with a fox was relevant. So, Wilf allowed Torture Tuesday to pass normally and didn't mention ocelots once.

On his Wednesday *Metro* round, he sat outside the three Toms' houses. English Tom came out and, seeing Wilf, crossed the street. Wilf waited.

Tom had a swinging limp. He'd taken a bullet in his hip on military service, many decades ago. It was still wedged there.

As he grew into his eighties, his limp seemed to widen. He walked sloping up and down with each step, but still like a soldier. Still obsessed with attractive women, who he gawped at in the streets unembarrassed. To him, all women were attractive.

'Alright, Wilf? You hear about Luca?'

'What?' asked Wilf, suddenly alarmed.

'They're saying it's a hit man. They're saying his family took out a contract, to get at his millions.'

'Who?'

'Y'know, coppers outside his house. They're saying it was a professional killing.'

Wilf didn't know how to react.

'I . . . don't think so,' said English Tom. 'Tell you what. They've let black-on-black crime run riot. It spills over when you ignore it.'

'That's racist,' said Wilf, thinking of Felicia.

'How can I be racist after all the black women I've slept with?' asked English Tom.

Wilf, despite himself, almost laughed. He realised he liked English Tom, though Felicia said he was a misogynistic bigot.

'Take me as you find me or take a hike, pal,' added Tom.

Wilf stood up to go.

'I didn't mean literally. Anyway, Brexit is clearing out the foreigners.'

'Politics,' said Wilf, contemptuously, and walked away.

Later, when he spoke to Felicia, she rolled up her eyes, then told him about the swirl of Luca rumours. Luca was, in descending order of popularity, killed by a gay lover, a mugger, a drive-by, an opportunist serial killer, and a hit man.

Wilf breathed a sigh of relief.

At home, relaxed again, he started his evening with Oscar Wilde. He grew absorbed, re-reading the same sentences. When Oscar was in prison in 1895, he didn't like the diet of gruel and suet, but tolerated the soup. He often went hungry. Wilf reflected that maybe Reading Gaol Wilde was not the same man as Tite Street Wilde. Oscar had changed too, like him. He went from behind nets to behind bars. He found a way to resist hunger, as Wilf at times had to do.

As light dimmed, Wilf looked forward to a night with his pet.

Suddenly, there was a bang on the corrugated metal of his front door. Then a succession of bangs.

Wilf stayed stock still.

The bangs started again. Then a brief pause. Then more.

He silently coasted through the hall to the door and looked through the eye vent.

It was the police. A squad car light was flashing.

He felt terrified. He raced back and forth to his kitchen in alarm.

PART 2
THE YEW ROAD SIEGE

65

DETECTIVE Inspector Steve Solomon was a time pauper. Overloaded with murder, he rarely had a moment to himself.

Earlier that day, in a few seconds of coffee break, he had glanced at the newest police recruitment brochure. Its cover displayed a group of smiling multicultural bobbies.

It read, 'if you rise to detective, you'll usually work on several cases at the same time.' Why didn't it tell the truth? Several dozen.

He was working on four gangland shootings, two stabbing deaths, a body in King Edward Park, suspicious deaths in Harlesden, Wembley and Colindale, two likely drug overdoses, and a hit-and-run. This morning, he'd seen a teen boy dead, gashed on the head. Probably with a machete.

Before leaving for work, he'd stooped to kiss his own boy, awake in his cot. He grinned at the baby's attempt at words. 'Bao . . . wao . . . ii.' fourteen months old and already a Bowie fan.

He kissed the big, lush forehead again. The high point of his day.

When the forensics came in that evening on the Luca Vignal stabbing, he felt a scintilla of strain lift from his shoulders. There was a clear match on the prints from the scarf. The suspect had been arrested in the past.

He looked up the files.

Wilfred Kelly, aka "Wilf", lived in the same tree streets as Vignal. He seemed like a sad case.

As he watched the formal police interview with the clearly disturbed man on video, he wondered why nobody had ever helped him. If only someone had intervened sooner, Luca Vignal might still be alive.

He felt sorry for Kelly but decided to pull him in right away.

He didn't expect any trouble, so took a regular panda car with Padma and Eric, two of the duty uniforms.

They drew up at a house that was possibly the worst in Brent borough. In the centre of the neat terrace of Yew Road, it oozed cracks and lichen upwards on dislocating bricks. The gate post was tilting over. When he went to look closer, he saw corrugated sheets on the door, ragged dirty curtains, cardboard, glimpses of junk.

When he bent over the splitting wall outside, he saw a worm.

Disgusted, he turned around and gave a bang on the door.

66

FELICIA heard the noise. It was the quiet time of evening, when her grandchildren had just been guided to bed.

Looking through the curtains, she froze in shock. Police were outside Wilf's house. A car with flashing lights stood with its wing between his bins, in his mum's hallowed spot.

She watched as a cop in plain clothes banged Wilf's door with his fist. Two junior cops were posted outside the gate.

Felicia forgot her fibroids and rushed over at lightning speed.

'What are you doing?' she hissed between the shoulders of the two uniforms who blocked her.

'Who are you?' asked DI Solomon.

'Felicia O'Dwyer. I'm his neighbour. Leave him alone.'

'I'm glad you're here,' said DI Solomon. He'd read her statement in the suspect's file and felt she might be helpful, though on seeing her in person, he wasn't so sure. She looked like trouble. 'Do you know where Mr Kelly is?'

'He's in there.'

'Why won't he answer the door?'

'He never answers his door. You're wasting your time.'

'Can *you* make him answer?

'What part of never's a fucking mystery? Leave him alone.'

'Thanks for your help. Felicia, isn't it? Go back home, please, indoors.'

The uniforms ushered her back onto the road. She watched DI Solomon get into the police car, switch off its blinking lights, tap on his smartphone and start a discussion.

When she turned to her house, her entire family were outside. Her son Vince was smoking one of his three-skin joints and gave her a grin. Her daughter Aoife had her back turned, taking a selfie with cops behind her. Her grandkids, Vince Jr. and Lucy, in their pyjamas, had clearly been told, 'Stay quiet or you'll go back to bed.'

'Is Worzel in trouble again?' asked Vince.

His mother jabbed him in the chest.

'Don't - call - him - Wor - zel.'

'Sorry, Ma. What do you want me to do?'

'Get people out here.'

67

VINCE jumped to it right away. He strode down the street, whipping his phone out.

Aoife took sentinel duty. She guided the kids back in and to their beds, then stood at the front bedroom window, filming with her phone. She borrowed Vince's long charger lead, to keep it powered.

Felicia went into her house. When Wilf had been arrested years before, it left him in a state of petrified fear. For weeks, Vince had to fetch groceries to leave outside his door. But Wilf, being Wilf, had finally ventured out to feed pigeons.

She swore she would never let him suffer like that again. DI Solomon had been right - she was trouble.

She found her old un-smart Nokia phone, with its tiny screen where she could scroll memorised numbers. She thought about who to call first. There was only one answer: Professor Emma.

After speaking with Emma, she phoned Ana, the Czech cop.

Then she phoned the poet Kevin Curran, who lived in Number 3.

Then she phoned the three Toms, English Tom, the slowest, first, Bulfast Tom, the fastest, last.

Everyone in the tree streets knew Wilf. She was spoilt for choice when it came to who to call next.

Ray Houghton? He was far too shy to want to be involved. But he wrote for the *Times*, he knew people. She gave him a bell, and his mild voice answered. She explained the situation.

'Oh dear,' he said. 'I'll call my friend Brian and see if he can come with a photographer.'

When Felicia ended the call, she went outside and looked up the street. In the centre of Yew Road, Professor Emma was in full throttle on her chair, taking the speed bumps effortlessly. She saw the three Toms emerging, with their two wives.

Felicia looked the other way. Youths had drifted onto that side, not all especially young, but dressed in ways suggestibly so. These were Vince's Bros. Felicia sensed he used that word loosely because he wasn't always sure which were true friends. But they all made money together, running food stalls at Notting Hill Carnival, doing security jobs at pubs, dealing a little weed now and then or, like Vince, doing painting and decorating for cash-in-hand. Some of them played music gigs and the Kellett twins were actors.

Rather than walk along the street, the Bros fanned apart to knock on one door after another. She saw one gesturing a couple out and pointing at the police car.

She thought of calling Beardy Callum, who always needed news stories for money. Sadly, she decided if he came, he'd be the first one arrested. The Scot couldn't bear injustice.

68

WHEN Professor Emma arrived, the two uniformed officers, Padma and Eric, stepped aside. It was a mark of respect but also an observation of guidelines concerning the differently abled. Also, neither wanted to get their knees rammed by an over-revved wheelchair.

Emma spurted forward and in an arc reversed her chair skilfully through Wilf's gateway, to his front door.

By this time, all three Toms had caught up. They linked arms outside Wilf's gate and stood in a crescent, chests forward. The two officers were cognizant of age, so were reluctant to touch them. Also, two women drifted across.

'Careful, now,' said Mayo Tom.

The uniforms glanced at each other, seeming like they wanted to confer, but Maureen distracted Padma by asking her name and enquiring, 'Is it rules to keep your hair pinned back like that?'

DI Solomon got out of the police car. He leaned against its roof and looked at what was going on around him. He realised he'd created a situation.

He felt like slamming his head on the car roof.

Professor Emma spoke up.

'If you plan to use brutality, legs only, please. Leave the face alone.'

He climbed back inside the vehicle and got on his phone again. He needed reinforcements.

69

A lot of people had emerged from their homes now and were walking towards Wilf's house. Some were making phone calls. Felicia was joined by Ana and Kevin Curran. Ana wasn't wearing her engagement ring, and Felicia wondered if she'd quarrelled with her fiancé. But the Czech was as unreadable as ever. Kevin's hair needed a combover. The three discussed the problem. Ana had brought her police ID. She nodded and walked towards DI Solomon.

Kevin said, 'Are you sure you want this online?'

'I want to put pressure on the cops, to get them away from Wilf's door.'

'You know, if I do anything, I'll get arrested.'

'Are you a virgin arrestee, Kev?'

'No,' he said. 'They have to let me out in two weeks. By law. I don't want to brood on what happens in most countries.'

Kevin grinned and took out his phone. He had a boyish love of mischief, despite knowing what police cells felt like.

He lifted his phone, tapped his finger on a screen icon to start livestreaming and said aloud to followers, 'Yo y'all, and shout out. Special episode podcast, timestamp now. This is what happens when we're overrun by force. This is tonight, Yew Road, London, a disabled man barricaded in his home, besieged by police. His crime, not answering his door.'

Kevin had begun to sidle along the road, filming. He was Americanising his accent, as if to harmonise with a global audience.

Felicia left him to it. It sounded like he knew what he was doing.

70

WILF, meanwhile, was sitting at the bottom of his stairs.

He heard Felicia's voice, then the banging on his door stopped. It felt like when she used to stay with him after his mum went out, if he fell asleep. She hissed like that if his mum came home too loudly. She knew he didn't like being woken up.

He decided to go upstairs, to peep out his mum's bedroom window for a bird's eye view of Yew Road.

He felt perspiration.

He heard a soft padding and his fox trotted into the hall and snuffled darkly at the front door. He could sense it indecisive, its forepaws twitching.

It had come naturally to be with him. It felt like fox love.

But he wished they could be elsewhere, in the thicket beside Speranza's grave, in the Saatchi, anywhere. As he turned to go up the stairs, he remembered a question his mum once asked, when feeling tired and achy, taking off her shoe to rub her foot, in her Waterford way.

'A good feed, heat, sleep, they're the best things in life. The rest . . . what do you think life is, Wilf?'

'Osmosis.'

He climbed stairs. He heard a siren.

71

OUTSIDE, Ana had shown her Metropolitan Police warrant card and spoken a long time to DI Solomon.

She peeled off and walked over to Felicia, her face solemn. By now groups of people were backing aside to let cars pass. One of these was a blaring police car that pulled into a space nearby, depositing three more uniforms. A cop leaned back to the dashboard to turn the siren off.

'They want to question him about Luca's murder,' said Ana.

'WHAT?'

'They found his fingerprints at the scene.'

In shock, Felicia stared over at DI Solomon, who was talking to the new cops.

'I want a word with that man.'

Ana gave a considered pause, then went and spoke to the DI, who gestured Felicia to him.

'Thanks for helping us,' he said, without irony.

'How did you get Wilf's fingerprints?' she demanded.

Solomon glanced at Ana, with a clear expression of betrayal.

'He was arrested a number of years ago.'

'I know. He never told me you fingerprinted him.'

The DI didn't respond. His eyes twitched slightly left and right, evasively.

'He shouldn't have been arrested,' said Felicia.

'It was a sex offence. He exposed himself to children outside a playground.'

'No, he didn't. His belt snapped but he kept his trousers up.'

'That's not what a witness said.'

'But not the kids. They just said Smelly Kelly nearly fell over.'

'It was a nanny doing her job.'

'And you believed one person?'

'He was outside a playground. He was only held forty-eight hours.'

'Do you have any idea of the damage you did?'

Felicia felt Ana's firm hand descend on her shoulder, to calm her down.

'Why were prints not destroyed?' she asked, citing police procedure. 'If no charges were brought.'

'I don't know,' said DI Solomon. 'They stayed on file. I don't know why.'

He looked at Felicia. 'If you can't help, please step back. This is a murder enquiry.'

'Wilf wouldn't harm anyone.'

She was ushered away from the scene by Ana, Padma and Eric, before she could offer actual help.

72

THERE were a lot more people now. Both sides of Yew Road were filling up.

Felicia heard a tutting sound coming closer from above. She looked up. It was a helicopter. She heard more sirens and looked along the street. Flashing lights were arriving on the ball court side. It was a police mini-bus. Shortly after, she saw a second mini-bus arrive on the Beech Road side.

Ana came over and said, 'They want to cordon off the area. They want everyone to go home. I'm to persuade you.'

'What should I do?'

'Do you have loudspeaker? How can you tell people to go? I can't persuade you . . . it has a life of its own now.'

It was true. Families were still coming from their houses. A thin stream of newcomers were edging around the street corners. She saw people distantly appear on the Green. More sirens were approaching from different directions.

A lot of her neighbours wanted to have personal words and made moves towards her, but she waved them back.

'What's police procedure?' she asked Ana.

'They run down the channels, both sides of street. When they get here, they form lines across, and work crowd back.'

Felicia looked both sides and did begin to see uniforms hurrying along the garden walls.

'It's not riot police,' said Ana. 'They don't have shields. That's later.'

A few police officers arrived and moved sideways in front of the crowd, waving their palms down gently for calm.

'Standard training while you wait back up,' explained Ana, admiringly. 'British police tactic. In Prague, we just hit them.'

'Ana, will Wilf get hurt?'

'No, no. I'll arrest him. The DI has agreed. I won't let anyone hurt him.'

'Thanks.'

'Wilf will walk in an hour. My senior got the arrest warrant after he came.'

Hearing that, Felicia immediately reached for her phone and rang Eileen, the Texan lawyer.

73

THE police formed a cordon on both sides, exactly as Ana predicted, and coaxed people back. Yew Road was civilised and respectful. Though concerns were raised, a few neighbours began to peel away and go home.

Felicia watched them, seeing the light from doors opening and closing.

But one man skipped inside the cordon and strode up the centre of the road on easy feet, alone, with a guitar slung on his back.

It was Island Garth.

He arrived where he wanted to be, outside Wilf's house. Felicia and Ana stepped back a pace, Ana signalling 'please, no' to DI Solomon.

Garth heaved his guitar to the front. It had strings. He took up position with his legs and shoulders, as if on stage, and after a few tuning strums, twanged a profound, agile rhythm.

He began to sing.

He sang 'Redemption Song,' by Bob Marley. He sang loud in his chokey, West Indian song voice, towards Wilf's windows. Everyone on the street fell quiet. Even the chopper sound swerved to a fading percussion.

Felicia listened until she heard him repeat the powerful lyrics about emancipation from mental slavery. Then she went over.

'Garth, you'll get into trouble.'

She gestured towards the police.

'They're waiting for an excuse to grab somebody.'
'They can grab this,' said Garth, grasping the front of his trousers.
'Wilf doesn't care what's down there, but your guitar, he would.'
'Don't get it broken.'
'Keep it safe,' said Felicia.

Island Garth assented, nodding, shouting 'Here for Wilf' at the windows and pumping his fist, knowing Wilf heard him.

As he walked home, people seemed to emerge again, emboldened. More arrived from both ends of the street.

She even saw Big Don and Norris, helping his mum.

74

THE first reporter arrived.

A man escorted by a petite photographer wearing a wrap-around hip cloth and T-shirt reading, KANGA GIRL, had wormed their way to the front of the crowd, now pressing against the police line.

'Brian Tomkins, *Times*,' he called out. 'Are you Felicia? Do you know Ray Houghton?'

The woman took photos as Felicia came over. She felt unattractive and lumpy, in her older slacks. Also, she now had misgivings, about the scale of this. Could she have handled it more diplomatically?

'So, what's going on, Felicia?' asked Brian, holding a phone in front of her. She realised it was recording. Reporters didn't use notebooks anymore.

Felicia composed herself and explained the situation.

She was open about Wilf's arrest, she knew that in a murder enquiry, it would be public anyway, a big deal. She told Brian she was to blame. She bought Wilf many belts, but he had a favourite one, in tatters, and it snapped at the wrong time in the wrong place.

She pointed out how isolated he must feel. He was vulnerable.

She deflected questions about his family. 'We're his family,' she said, meaning the tree streets people. 'We look after him.'

She suddenly realised what Wilf would say, if he was beside her right now. She almost heard him speak.

'What's a kanga?'

'It's what the photographer is wearing,' she would have explained, patiently.

75

AFTER the interview, Felicia watched the two journalists move around to ask questions of other people. Big Don shoved over to introduce himself.

She hadn't thought of that and was instantly worried. She decided to phone Ray again.

'Sorry for disturbing you,' she said as he answered.

'Oh, don't mention it. I'm watching through the window.'

'Brian's talking to Don, can you ask him to talk to someone else?'

'He will.'

Felicia waited while Ray said nothing. She genuinely expected him to say more. He didn't.

'Thanks,' she said.

That was unhelpful.

She decided to phone Beardy Callum after all, for alternative journalism. Then stopped herself, with a sudden thought, and instead phoned the Vicar of St. Aubert. He might be the one person who could talk Wilf out of his house.

As she spoke to him, she looked over at DI Solomon. He was looking at her, also speaking on his phone.

His was a personal call. He left a message for his wife. He apologised. It would be a long, drawn-out night. He might not get home. He imagined her sitting at the kitchen island, pouring a glass of wine.

'I've really messed up,' he confessed. 'I wish I was there with you.'

Suddenly, his wife picked up the phone. 'S'alright, Steve. I'll kiss Davy for you.'

DI Solomon imagined his infant son, in his cot, kicking his little legs in beat to a Bowie song, maybe Rebel Rebel. Davy loved it when music was turned up loud. They did little air dances together, with his fingers and his baby's tiny hands.

The thought made him feel human again, for an instant.

'I might lose my job over this one,' he said.

76

MORE police were arriving, almost as fast as the media vans. London hadn't seen a serious siege since terrorists occupied the Iranian Embassy in 1980. For the media, it was a bonanza.

People with shoulder cameras and microphones began infiltrating the crowd, which was still growing, with a mildly Carnival atmosphere.

Back at the centre of the action, Ana began to seem concerned. She sensed DI Solomon was too calm, almost nonchalant, speaking occasionally into a shoulder mike that one of the new cops had brought.

'He's up to something fishy,' she said, adding, 'even if he means well.'

'Find out what it is.'

Ana went over. Felicia watched an exchange of words. Ana's veneer changed and a moment of betrayal crossed her face, just as one had earlier on DI Solomon's. The DI got her to agree to something, and she nodded. She came back.

'Stay calm. He's pulled rank. He sent for an armed response unit. They're going in the back right now.'

'WHAT?' said Felicia.

'Too late. Keep our heads.'

Ana stared her older friend into silence, as per orders. Felicia felt frail and on the verge of tears. Ana stood tall like a barrier, police.

Felicia swung aside to Kevin Curran, who was on one of his slow hovers, speaking into his phone. She leaned her face into it.

'They're sending in SWAT. They'll shoot him.'

She swung back to Ana, who heard but said nothing. Felicia was working herself into a real rage now.

Suddenly DI Solomon spoke a word sharply into his shoulder: 'Abort'.

He looked hard at Felicia and Ana, before gesturing both over.

'Does Kelly have dogs?'

'No,' said Felicia, rudely.

'Our lead officer was attacked. He got bitten.'

'Good.'

'Could it be Kelly with a weapon?'

'No,' said Felicia. 'And, in case you're wondering, he doesn't run on all fours.'

After a pause, DI Solomon resumed in what he hoped was a de-escalating tone: 'We didn't want to panic him, so we withdrew.'

'I don't even have a response to that.'

Ana finally spoke. 'This is good news. Nothing happened.'

"I need head room,' said Felicia, breaking away.

She curved off into a few arcs and, as she swung by Kevin's phone, said:

'The hard men met Wilf's pear tree. They ran away.'

77

BUT that was the end of Kevin Curran's night.
Two well-dressed men had shown ID cards at the cordon and walked straight towards him.

'Kevin Curran?' asked one.

'MI6?' replied Kevin.

'You don't need to know. Hand over the equipment and follow us.'

'I won't make a scene,' said Kevin, offering his phone.

'Please turn it off.'

Kevin did so and then was threaded in single file through the crowd between the two men, with a final shout to Felicia.

'Garth's gone viral.'

78

THE crowd stretched both sides of Yew Road to the corners, spilling further. Arrivals came all the time from the train station, following live broadcasts on their phones.

It was almost with relief that DI Solomon decided to ring it into HQ as a major incident and request all available resources.

The area would need lockdown. Thankfully, there was a cemetery on one side. A natural border. Three sides left to secure.

He knew he would be relieved of command soon. They would rush over someone senior to deal with the media and on-the-ground protocol. He might be consigned to the punishment of home.

'It's like the Siege of Limoges,' he heard the wheelchair woman shout, almost ecstatically.

Supine Mario suddenly materialised by Felicia's shoulder. He was sober. He'd showered and brushed his hair but kept his sharing-a-secret look.

"S Wilf. I can help. I can go in the back, I'm good at this. Get 'im out, I don't have trouble with dogs.'

'Thanks but no, Mario, I don't think that's a good idea.'

"I'm Mr Invisible. I bring 'im later. 'S Wilfie. I hide 'im in my room. No drink, no smoke, everything normal.'

'Thanks. But can you watch the cops, Mario? I don't trust them. Tell me if they try . . . anything at all.'

She gave him a real hug, 'Thanks.'

Mario reminded her of Wilf, a genius for self-sabotage. And more intelligent than he seemed. He'd taught himself English, even though barely anyone in the tree streets learnt a word of his language in return.

'I stay,' he promised.

He stepped behind Felicia to the kerb, ready to get between her and a cop.

It felt like the most supportive moment of her entire night.

She heard her name called in a rasping voice. She looked over and saw Eileen the Texan held back at the cordon by a policeman.

79

DI Solomon tried to reason with the three men shielding the gate, especially the smallest in the centre, who looked the most pliable. They were, he pointed out, making Wilf's situation worse by prolonging it.

'Wilf won't mind,' said Mayo Tom. 'He'd rather be in there than out here.'

'He doesn't have our sense of time,' added the big man with the Northern Irish accent. 'His lasts longer.'

'Safe inside or banged up outside,' said the oldest. 'What choice would you make, mate?'

'And don't ask the women's opinion,' chipped in Professor Emma, from behind them.

'O sa babaeng Asyano,' added Maja, in Tagalog.

The DI finally had to accept reality. To arrest Wilf, he needed to win these people over. He consulted with Ana and finally called Felicia.

He readied himself for diplomacy, but she said instantly, pointing at a woman being held back by the police cordon:

'Bring her here. She's with Wilf.'

The DI ordered the new woman to be escorted over, hoping it might be a good thing, especially if romance. What was meant by "with"?

As she approached, he noticed she had a nose ring. So maybe in Kelly's same weird zone? Maybe, a real thing?

"I'm Eileen MacNamara of Dillon Lance. I'm here to give Wilf Kelly legal support. Why are you harassing him?'

He felt the humiliation of being wrong again.

'Mr. Kelly is needed for questioning in connection with a murder,' he replied patiently.

'Let me see your arrest warrant.'

DI Solomon scrolled through his mobile phone. He showed her his power-of-entry warrant.

'You arrived before then,' said Ana, innocently.

'I came to make initial enquiries.'

'Did he know that?' asked Eileen. 'Did you say, "this is the police"?'

DI Solomon knew he was on solid ground. He got the warrant before he called in an armed response unit. This was cobwebs.

'I'm concerned for Wilf's safety. Please listen.'

They did. They all fell quiet.

'How can I get him out?'

'That's easy,' said Felicia. 'He'll come out himself to deliver the *Metro*.'

80

THE DI could scarcely believe what he next heard. Wait for Kelly to go for a newspaper? Tomorrow morning?

The DI had been bullied at school. But he'd taught himself small breathing exercises, for before and after trouble. Breathing control later proved beneficial to his sex life too, but now he used it to keep his mind cold and clear.

He had seen Wilf Kelly with his own eyes, on video. Kelly was a man who, when asked if he exposed himself to kids, said, 'Hrymmphh.' Then, asked if he felt drawn to kids in some way, said, 'Taps you can't turn off,' which led to a puzzled pause in the interviewing duo. One asked if there were things he ever thought of doing to kids? He said, 'Give them the *Metro*.'

To Wilf, this made perfect sense. If he gave the kids a gift, their gift back might be no more mockery. Though that was improbable.

DI Solomon was not looking forward to interviewing him. He'd need a therapist in the room, for his personal benefit, not Wilf's. He wished he could be relieved of duty.

Felicia repeated again and again that Wilf wouldn't come out till morning. She insisted that the street must seem normal, nobody could be here.

'Not going to happen,' he said.

'He's capable of staying in there a month.'

'Can you get rid of the helicopters at least?' asked Eileen. 'They don't help.'

'Wilf won't slip out the back,' promised Ana. 'He won't run.'

There were now three choppers clattering above. The pair swooping lowest were News.

'That's a good idea,' conceded Solomon. 'Get the alarm level down. I'll call it in. Now, as regards the newspaper . . . we can't wait. The crowd is too big. It's a safety risk. We have to bring him out. Why can't one of you call through the door and ask him to speak?'

'He never answers his door,' explained Felicia patiently.

'It's not impossible to clear the streets,' said Ana.

'We can help,' said Felicia, immediately catching Ana's drift. 'We can ask people to go home or get out of sight.'

'And the media?'

'If anyone knows how to stay out of sight till the shittiest moment, the media do,' rasped Eileen.

'I'll make the arrest,' said Ana. 'We agreed. He trusts me.'

'Let him finish his *Metro* round first,' said Professor Emma, defiantly.

'Hear, hear,' said English Tom.

Felicia waved her friends quiet.

'No, not possible,' decided DI Solomon. 'Too big a risk. I'm sorry, you'll have to think of another way or we break in.'

'Past them?' asked Felicia, nodding towards Emma and the Toms.

'Past them.'

'If that happens,' threatened Eileen, 'this goes upstairs to the Minister of State for Care and Mental Health. Do you want to know her name?'

'No,' said DI Solomon.

'My firm donates to her party.'

'What if we all ask him to come out?' piped up Mayo Tom, unexpectedly.

DI Solomon turned to look at the central pillar of the three Tom post. He nodded approvingly.

A shimmer of consensus went around, until Felicia shattered it by saying: 'Won't work. He's afraid of the dark.'

Oh, please, thought DI Solomon.

'Wilf,' yelled Professor Emma suddenly. 'Come out, love. It's Emma.'

A wave of quiet spread. They waited. She jerked her chair forward.

'Wilf. C'mon out, please.' After a while, more like herself, 'Bring a book, we'll read it in the paddy-wagon together.'

She jerked back.

'I thought it was worth a try,' she said.

'Not helpful, Emma,' said Ana in her police voice.

Felicia was scrolling through some texts.

'Wait. There's . . . a Plan B. A local vicar is trapped down the road. He might get Wilf to talk. They have a bond. He was close to Wilf's mum. He gave her funeral service.'

'Okay,' said DI Solomon, 'let's get him here.'

'And if it doesn't work?'

'All right,' he conceded. 'If it doesn't work, we'll wait for him to come out in the morning.'

In his mind, he prayed that Wilf was deeply religious.

81

DRAWING away, he issued orders to his officers and raised HQ to deal with the helicopters.

Felicia phoned the Vicar, asking him to make himself known to a police officer. While on the phone, she looked towards her own house. Her daughter Aoife was at the window, filming. Felicia tapped her fingers to her lips and rose them towards her. Aoife did likewise back. Family first.

It took nearly ten minutes for the Vicar to squeeze through. A uniform laid a hand firmly on a youth's head to hold him back while he wriggled past the last shoulders. The photographer snapped it.

The Vicar's ponytail was wound up into a Japanese bun. He made himself orderly, adjusting his clerical collar. He wore jeans downstairs. He closed his eyes an instant, to zone himself in internal peace, thinking of the quietness inside St. Aubert's Church.

He joined the group at Wilf's gate, surprised to see a woman in a wheelchair blocking the front door. He knew her, but couldn't quite remember her name, a teacher or a lecturer. Felicia introduced him around and they spoke in quiet voices. They were joined by

DI Solomon, who shook his hand. They conferred a while longer.

Finally, the three Toms broke their chain and Professor Emma purred away. The Vicar was now alone, centre stage.

Wilf Kelly, inside this house, was the son of a woman he'd loved very dearly, for years. The only test of his marriage. He'd watched him as a child from tottering age never looking him in the face. One time, his mum led her finger from Wilf's eyes to his, and they locked gaze an instant. Something in that gaze make him feel that Wilf was not hopelessly different. The boy knew what was around him.

'He's very, very intelligent,' said Wilf's mum, adding, to Wilf, 'my little brainbox.'

But in all the years since, he never learned how to talk to Wilf as his mum or Felicia could. After the funeral, Wilf once came to sit in the church, and he sat alongside for a long time. They didn't speak.

He was not sure what to say now, either. He noticed a crack between the door's metal sheets and approached.

He peered through it. He saw movement. He felt sure Wilf was on the stairs. Another movement. It was Wilf. He could see his shape. A shred of light glimmered from the kitchen. He wished he had a torch to shine through but realised it would be horrifying for the man inside.

He put his lips to the vent and said quietly: 'Wilf?'

He waited.

'Wilf. Can we talk?'

Wilf didn't reply. But this was not unusual. Wilf had spurts of talking but a lot more of not.

'I'm sending the police away. It's all a mistake.'

He waited.

'It's okay.' Then after a while, 'Please, Wilf. Talk to me.'

He waited.

'Wilf, you like people. You told me. You can trust me.'

He waited.

Finally, he was left with the oldest tactic in his playbook, the one that nearly always brought at least a 'Hrymmphh': 'What do you think of God now?'

Wilf replied the way God normally did.

The Vicar finally stepped away. He pulled back into the street and scanned the house front. He looked hard at the door. Suddenly, he had a powerful feeling that Wilf was right, nobody should force him from his home, ever, unless in his own time.

'You have rights, Wilf,' he shouted.

'You have rights.'

Oh, please, thought DI Solomon.

A slow handclap started. People began chanting, 'You have rights.' The chant spread along both sides of Yew Road. 'You have rights.'

A counter-chant broke out, 'Here for Wilf.'

After a brief jostle, 'Here for Wilf' overtook 'You have rights' and left it dusting off into the distance. The street was a sea of chants.

The Vicar strode into the centre of the road and cut them out, with a few waves. It took him a few turns each side slowly to gain quiet.

'Wilf,' he shouted, facing the house. 'We're all going home. It's okay.'

He paused, trying to think of something final to say.

'Good night to you, mister.'

As he walked away, he gestured everyone to leave, stopping and explaining why to smaller groups.

The police waved the public back. Their vehicles slowly reversed. Felicia moved around, with Eileen and Ana, explaining and urging people to go. Very quickly, Vince's Bros began mingling and speaking too. Emma with the Toms and their wives worked in the opposite direction.

As on the ground people retreated, the distant but steady blade noises overhead swayed into no noise.

82

SLOWLY, slowly, Yew Road was abandoned.

Most neighbours went home. Felicia knew they would be setting alarms for early in the morning to take up positions behind windows.

But around the four corners, behind cordons, a swell of people, outsiders, were kept back by more and more police, arriving in relays in vehicles drawing up by the playground, where no swings swung.

Kevin really had been effective. She heard Garth's song from a lot of phones.

Ana told her that trains were no longer stopping at the local station, by police orders, for crowd control.

'But, you know, nobody can go home either,' she observed drily.

Everything was quiet. In a rare show of imagination, the police had got hold of large sheets of flipboard paper, and wrote in fat crayon, PLEASE BE QUIET.

They held up the paper, awkwardly, flapping. As each cop got a sheet, they strode away, speaking quietly and explaining the need for calm.

Everywhere the word was spread, please be quiet. It was going to be a long night.

83

THE community garden got ruined.

Police trampled on it as they edged out a camera from the strip between the ball court and the pavement. They spiked the camera on a low trident, silently recording. An older officer sat against the wall to ensure nobody stole it.

Eileen surveyed the mess sadly, wondering who she might rope in to help dig it up again and plant new roots. Of her two fellow gardeners, Oliver was reliable, but Marcus's time was tied up colourising a 1930s Cary Grant film for Netflix. She gave both of them a ring, only to find they were somewhere in the crowd. It felt good to talk to them.

Streets were thronged. People in groups or singly wandered on Birch Road, Beech Road, Elm Road, Oak Road, anywhere arboreal but Yew. A fire was started on the Green and youngsters sat around it. Only when bottles or cans appeared did police quietly move in. They requested no drinking, and finally they allowed people to leave bags or containers of booze in the ball court for collection afterwards.

The ball court was now police central.

Its gates were open. Vans were dotted in the play area, including an ambulance. Uniforms came in and out or stood in briefing groups. There was a van of electronic gear, lights. Laptops were set up on a folding table, fed video from surveillance cameras (more were set up at the far end of Yew Road). The van also had folding chairs, for which DI Solomon made a beeline.

He took an extra chair for Felicia, who was looking tired and heavy. She plonked herself down and lifted her sore feet one at a time.

'Thanks.'

It was going to be a long night.

The diner on Harrow Road corner had opened its doors for beverages and snacks. Its owner pulled out a trolley with a coffee vat and dragged it wobbling into the ball court. He offered free hot drinks to the officers. Di Solomon was humble enough to stand in line with the others.

He fetched two cups and came back to Felicia, sitting down to talk.

She began warming to him. He was ordinary but melancholic. Dark shadows from sleeplessness were spreading under his eyes. He was a soft-spoken Tottenham man who worked too hard. Just as exhausted as she was on his folding chair, drinking his coffee black.

She began to probe out details about him. Father of an infant son.

He worried about late nights like this, because after putting Davy down, his wife liked to relax with a glass of wine. She was a brilliant mother, and juggled Davy with a flexitime job at an architects' office, but had low resistance. One drink sometimes led to another.

Felicia probed.

His wife had been drunk when he first met her, coming across her after a hen's night party. Separated from her ally hens, she'd fallen asleep in a pub car park, on her back in a mini skirt, legs sprawled, knees in the air.

'Her face wasn't the first thing I noticed.'

'White, red or black?'

'White.'

'She was sending out a call sign for a knight in shining armour.'

'Wrong, on so many counts,' he sighed.

'My experience of booze, as a woman, is the same as your wife's. I drink more if anyone hassles me about it. I have two great kids. If you don't nag her, your Davy'll grow up to surprise you. Mine did.'

They went quiet for a while.

'What'll happen to Wilf?'

'I don't know,' he said. 'I'm sorry, I've got to charge him.'

'He wouldn't hurt anyone.'

'It's for the Crown Prosecution Service to decide.'

'Crown Persecution, you mean, targeting the black and vulnerable. Let's not mention women.'

He thought it best not to engage on this so said: 'He'll spend a few days in a remand cell, then . . . maybe, a hospital or clinic.'

'And how will that help? It proves everything he's ever felt. Poke, poke, poke, that's what people do. We're hostile.'

DI Solomon wondered if she had ever given a speech. It seemed like she'd be good at it. He decided to nod, holding eye contact professionally, to defuse rising feelings.

'I'm sorry,' apologised Felicia. 'I don't mean to take it out on you. I mean, I'm going to take it out. It'll be a long night.'

84

IT was.

Night sailed above London.

While it did so, Felicia drank coffee. DI Solomon brought her another cup.

Meanwhile, on the tree streets, small dramas unfolded privately. A stranger to the area named Glen proposed to a woman named Gloria. They'd met on the Tube from South Kenton after separately hearing a protester on their TikTok feeds singing a Bob Marley song in defiance of police. Both came to join the protest. Now, the atmosphere swept Glen into intense love-at-first-sight emotions, so he proposed. Gloria accepted. They listened again to 'Redemption Song'.

On Oak Road, another stranger named Ely Moran didn't so much announce he was gay, as put his hand in his friend's, Chris's.

A lot of strangers began chatting to each other. Some ended up exchanging phone numbers.

On Birch Road, a man with a Waterford tattoo rested his hands on his rattling front gate. I've got to fix this yoke, he thought.

Ana the Czech prowled.

She prowled across the Green, past the youths at the fire and two men sharing a joint in the trees, along the path with smells from the dog poop bin, emerging by the train station. A few people were clustered at its gate waiting for a chance to go home.

She went over and told them it wouldn't open till morning.

Night was passing.

Beardy Callum was forced in front of a Desk Sergeant in Paddington Green Police Station, where normally terrorists were held. When he'd tried to shoulder his way up Yew Road to see Wilf, he felt a cop grip his dress and reacted. He was astonished by how fast he was dragged away and had to sit a long time in a caged police van. It felt like the British constabulary had been trained by Cuban instructors.

Kevin Curran was downstairs in the same station, answering questions.

English Tom went off on his own. He swung himself carefully onto the grass on the Green, let his weight down and sat, then gawped, in his rude way, at a woman a few yards away. She kept turning her profile. Her lips spoke words too far away to hear, but the shapes they made were like memories of sex in motion.

Night was passing.

Things were happening everywhere, quietly.

Big Don put his arm around Norris's Mum, supporting her. She'd stayed out searching for Norris, who'd gone off, as usual. Her leg was giving way and the police stopped her going to her home on Yew Road. Gently, Big Don guided her to his own house on Elm Road, to watch it all on the TV.

Felicia brooded silently. She'd given Wilf cheap mobile phones, twice. She'd sent Vince over to show him how they worked.

They ended up in his bin, like books. There was no way to call him.

He must be terrified.

Night wore on.

Mayo Tom and Maureen took a walk and talked about the diversity of the crowds, all ages, all colours, even a few families. 'I'd say,' said Tom finally, 'the police didn't expect this turnout.'

Professor Emma buzzed over to a uniform, on the ball court corner. 'Can you get me in there?' nodding to the court. The uniform spoke on his radio, and guided her through, over uneven cobbles at the entrance. She zeroed in on Felicia and drove up beside her.

'Hi. What's the latest?'

'We're drinking coffee,' said DI Solomon, 'do you want some?'

'Milk, two sugars.'

He went to fetch it. Emma and Felicia exchanged a few words and grew quiet.

Night wore on.

'They should have brought Port-a-Loos,' said Emma, observantly.

'Wouldn't fancy seeing what's happening in the bushes right now.'

'Do you need . . . ?'

'I'm fine.'

Bulfast Tom was exhausted so lay on his back in bed. His wife kissed him gently and snuggled her head in the nook of his shoulder, curling. He felt so much love, his arm squeezed her a tiny bit closer, sensing her.

Supine Mario stayed in sight of Felicia but was kept out of the ball court by police. He saw a friend – Djer – funny name, nearby. He went to talk.

Night sailed glacially.

Paulie Carson bumped into Vince, Felicia's son. Vince was younger, but respectfully invited him to mingle with the Bros, who were nearby.

Susan Carson, his twin sister, was alone and close to tears. She walked streets, edging thinly out of the way of people and police, and felt, if Wilf were here, she would know what to say. She wanted to tell him people cared about him. She wanted to hold him.

Night seemed to last forever.

Ray who wrote for the *Times* finally left his house. It was 36 Yew Road. He walked briskly to the corner, with police waving arms. He wasn't sure if they wanted him to go faster or turn back, so he went faster and saw Felicia stand up as he got in sight of the ball court. She waved him over and police stepped aside to let him in.

'Sorry about Brian,' he said.

'It's okay.'

'I should have called someone a bit more mature.'

Around then, night gave way to day's return journey.

85

LIGHT came fast at this time of year. Felicia saw it lift over roofs and felt it warm her face.

'It'll be a fine day,' intoned Ray. 'Mushroom picking weather.'

'Ray,' said Professor Emma, 'we need to make ourselves scarce.'

Ray, nothing if not intelligent, understood. He followed her chair as she drove over to the corner of the ball court and swung round.

'We can't interfere in the arrest,' she said.

'I hope they won't hurt him,' he said.

Glancing over, he saw DI Solomon and Felicia go to a table with laptop screens. A uniform set out a folding chair for Felicia. Ana, who'd arrived hurriedly, strode over for orders. She'd swung back to the station for a *Metro*, but the delivery had been held up. Traffic was frozen on Harrow Road.

Instead, she used her phone to show DI Solomon the headline: YEW ROAD SIEGE. He inhaled deeply and released a breath. He felt relieved that it didn't read, COP SCREWS UP.

'When will he come out?'

'After cornflakes,' said Felicia.

'Wilf's regular,' said Ana. 'He feeds birds every day.'

'Where do birds suddenly come in?"

'Just wait,' said Felicia, 'it's still early.'

The trio looked at the live video of Yew Road. Nothing moved. It was a still life. They watched.

Birds? thought DI Solomon.

He felt down, downer, downer, mistake, mistake.

He checked in with HQ. They asked for an assessment on re-opening the station and, right away, he agreed. Commuters needed to get to work. He glanced at the time.

He wondered why he was still here. He'd expected to be relieved of command, hours ago. Then he figured. They needed a scapegoat.

Felicia looked over to see him glaring at her with a repressed expression.

'Trust Wilf,' she said.

'Are you sure he'll come out?'

'He's hot to trot every morning,' said Ana. 'Like clockwork.'

86

BUT Felicia wasn't as sure as she seemed.

She pictured Wilf hunkered in his kitchen. He'd be thinking things out, as always. He knew cops never go away. If he came out, it would be because he wanted to step into morning and look around. He wanted to be himself.

Felicia knew if Ana walked up the street, Wilf would wait, knowing. But if he saw a uniform, he'd scuttle back inside.

It wasn't all about the *Metro*. He had curiosity about the outside world. He could have spent decades stepping out of his back door, but always came out the front.

He always braved up to the world.

But she felt he might not this time. She thought of how he looked and sounded at her house a few weeks ago, asking for painkillers. He seemed so desperate.

She watched the video feed of Yew Road carefully. It was too quiet.

She stood up as she saw the laptop clock hit 6.45.

'I need to see the street,' she said, meaning not a screen.

DI Solomon and Ana followed her as she left the ball court and stood on its corner with Yew Road, peering up the street.

There was a remarkable silence.

Remarkable, because the area throbbed with crowds, and from the now open station more now came, seeing police officers hold up pieces of paper reading, PLEASE BE QUIET, as they emerged.

Even the traffic seemed muted.

'He won't come out,' announced Felicia.

'What?' said DI Solomon.

'No pigeons on the roofs. The crowds have scared them off. We need to clear all the streets to get the pigeons back.'

'Did you hear what you just said?' asked DI Solomon.

'Yes,' said Felicia. 'I'm stupid, aren't I?'

She turned to face everyone and announced: 'I'll get him out.'

Abruptly, she strode up Yew Road. Ana jumped to keep pace and the DI spoke on his mike to hold everything back while gesturing Padma and Eric to follow. They broke out into a trot to catch up.

Felicia got to Wilf's door but didn't knock. She leaned forward and yelled through the vent, 'Are you coming out? You're pissing everyone off.'

She paused.

'Wilf Kelly, last chance, are you coming out?'

Silence.

'Break it down,' she said to DI Solomon, stepping back. 'There's something wrong.'

She expected Eric to put his foot through the door, or Padma her shoulder, but the DI radioed in a group of four men in helmets and stab jackets who raced up the street with a battering ram. She had to stand outside the gate while they rammed in the door with a collective thump.

An animal shot out and snapped its jaws at one of the cop's legs. It leapt in the air at another cop, snapping at his face, then swirled back inside, snarling, ready to attack, crouching to face them.

The cops fell back, dropping their ram. Felicia could see it was a red dog, at the end of the staircase, growling. She saw Wilf on the stairs behind it. He lay motionless on his front, in a rumpled jacket. It was one she'd bought for him recently, in Oxfam.

She closed her eyes and felt her head sway.

'It's a fucking fox,' said Ana.

87

DI Solomon pulled his team back. He radioed for paramedic support.

'Don't kill it,' said Felicia.

'I think it's best if you go home now,' said the DI.

'No.'

'I'll look after her,' said Ana.

DI Solomon put his hand gently on Felicia's shoulder. He felt her shrink back.

'I'm sorry,' he said.

'Don't kill it,' she pleaded.

Solomon recognised she was in shock.

When the paramedics arrived from the ball court, he asked one to keep an eye on her, in case she collapsed.

The paramedics couldn't enter the house. The fox feigned a lunge if anyone came near. It released a bark that sounded like a sort of soul-tortured banshee, jolting even him.

He called the RSPCA, rather than a police unit. A unit would be quicker, but shoot the fox. Civilian RSPCA would behave mindfully, ensuring Felicia's stability as much as dealing with the animal.

Then, he worked the lines to HQ to organise dispersal of the crowd. He thought of sheets of paper. They could say, WILF FOUND. He turned to Felicia, 'Can you help us clear the streets?'

She shook her head.

'Please, we need your help.'

'To do what?'

'Speak to that son of yours.'

Felicia pulled herself together. She took out her Nokia, almost whispering on it to Vince. She couldn't bring herself to say the words 'Wilf's dead,' but said, 'Wilf's hurt'. Could he get people to go home? Vince, no fool, sensed it was far worse. She could tell from his sombre tone as he said, 'Don't worry, Ma.'

After a time, a van with a blue RSPCA logo found its way through and drifted over the speed bumps on the deserted Yew Road. A young woman in blue coveralls emerged to assess the situation.

'Urban fox. Dog, healthy. Sorry, we'll have to put him down.'

'Why?' snapped Felicia instantly.

'Threatening behaviour,' explained the woman. 'Foxes aren't as vicious as their rep, but if he jumps, he can take off your lip. And they can do serious damage to a baby.'

'Why not release him in the country?' asked Ana.

'Territorial. He'll attack the local foxes. A fox somewhere is going to end up dead. I'm really sorry.'

She promised it would be painless. She'd tranquilise him and put him down humanely at base.

After looping back to the van, she approached with a long-snouted dart gun that looked like a selfie stick. She had put on surgical gloves.

But she didn't even make it to the gate.

Wilf's fox swirled suddenly from his hunched, threatening pose, bounded backwards and fled fast through the kitchen into the back garden.

It was as if he understood.

'Suspect's smart,' said Ana.

88

AFTER the paramedics confirmed Wilf's death, DI Solomon called in a crime scene team. He was sure this was no crime but decided to play everything by the rule book now.

Word came through from HQ that crowds were dispersing. They needed extra officers to control entry to the train station. The helicopters were back up, the police one radioing observations of swarms at bus stops.

People lined up outside the ball court to collect their booze.

Supine Mario and his friend Djer managed to bluff their way in and steal a few bags.

DI Solomon tried to persuade Felicia to go home to rest.

'No,' she said firmly.

Five minutes later, he instructed the crime scene manager to delay putting up tenting around Wilf's door.

'Just do the body work and get him out quick.'

He had to remind himself that Kelly was a murderer.

Felicia stood in stony silence. Ana was at her shoulder like a sister.

Padma and Eric shielded their view when the stretcher team finally got the go-ahead, turning Wilf's body heavily over, 1-2-3 hoisting him on his back onto the tilting stretcher.

Four of them bore him out to the ambulance, covered in a sheet. DI Solomon had instructed no body bag. They'd tucked the cloth around him with sensitivity. Nothing showed, not even footwear.

Not by the book, thought Ana. Possible scene contamination.

89

AFTER that, time seemed to accelerate.

DI Solomon took Felicia personally to Wembley Police Station for her statement. They had a silent car journey, Eric driving with Solomon alongside him, Felicia between Padma and Ana on the back seat.

Felicia broke the silence by asking, 'Do I need Eileen?'

'No,' said Ana. 'You're not under arrest.'

They fell silent again, cruising through the narrow channel of Wembley Central. Felicia felt crushed. This street was like a birth canal. She breathed a little deeper in relief as the road widened and Eric glided his way to the station.

DI Solomon led them inside.

He felt embarrassed by police interview rooms, designed for

discomfort, to encourage confessions. He thought there should be a tasteful room for victims and relatives. He'd even read about a project to paint walls pastel colours and install soft chairs and lighting, and felt it was a good idea.

Instead, he spent the next few hours sitting opposite Felicia and Ana in the best room available. He went through the paperwork, typing her statement onto a tablet.

He sent it to the printer. It took a short while. Padma brought in the print-out and Felicia read it over. Padma left a pen. She signed it.

'We'll take you home now,' said the DI. 'Try and get some rest.'

But Felicia refused to move.

'I want to know what happened to him?' she said.

'We don't know yet.'

'I want to know,' she repeated.

'We'll let you know as soon as possible.'

'I'm not in a hurry.'

She actually crossed her arms. Ana had to restrain a smile. Her old friend was re-emerging from stone.

'I take a guess,' she intervened. 'It's a big news story. I think autopsy might be there already.'

'I haven't heard,' said the DI.

Felicia's arms were really crossed. She had the glower of the Terminator.

'I'll ask them to get a move on.' He got up and left the room.

'I can't take anymore, Ana,' said Felicia, releasing her posture as soon as he was gone.

'You'll see,' said Ana. 'They'll tell us.'

The door opened again shortly afterwards, and DI Solomon came back inside. He was holding a phone. He put it on the table.

'This is Dr Eleanor Howe,' he said. 'She's signed Wilf's death certificate. She's on speaker.'

'Doctor?' Felicia asked towards the phone.

'Hello, are you Felicia? You want to know how Mr Kelly died. He had a brain haemorrhage. It would have been painless and quick.

Did you notice any changes in his behaviour? He may have had one or more mini strokes in the past.'

'No . . . he had a bad headache. I thought something happened. He wouldn't go to the doctor.'

'I understand. Felicia, it's not your fault. It was certain to happen anyway.'

The call ended and Felicia finally felt her face quiver. She drooped her head. Tears and heaves started to come.

She tried to stop.

Wilf would have called it a little girl wile.

But she couldn't stop. It came. She cried.

Later, after a cup of tea, she was driven home with Ana. The car returned with Ana to the police station. There would be debriefing, and then Solomon, Ana, Eric and Padma, might finally get home to sleep.

90

WILF'S fox made his escape through Number 4, Birch Road. This house was being renovated and was devoid of doors and windows. The fencing and canvas barriers were no barrier to him at all, and he glided through the house easily. As Wilf had guessed, a fox finds a way.

Birch Road was streaming with people. The fox ran.

He hugged the sides of parked cars and sprinted down the street, ears tucked back. He swerved to avoid a human leaning against a car, and swerved again to avoid human legs. A woman screamed.

'It's a fucking fox,' someone shouted.

Like a velvet mirage, he ran past the ball court, hugging its perimeter, and sped weaving through a thick forest of legs to the Harrow Road. He heard more human noises and a hand tried to touch him.

On the far side was the cemetery and he squeezed through its railings in a moment. He dropped his speed to a trot and found his way in among the graves.

Taking the path where he'd first met Wilf, he turned aside over a rough patch and entered the woods. At the base of a beech tree, his old den lay empty, though he could smell that rats had been in the vicinity. Sliding himself inside at a crouch, he entered the home where he'd been born. He curled himself into his brush and fell asleep from exhaustion.

91

LIKE Wilf's fox, burying her head in a pillow instead of a tail, Felicia lay still but couldn't sleep. She felt a profound sense of shock, of disbelief. Yesterday, Wilf was delivering *Metros*. Today, he was gone. It was all so sudden.

A deep guilt engulfed her, but she fought back against feeling responsible. She remembered his strangeness – his alert evasive eyes, how he stood, how he rocked himself forward and back, how he was keenly observant of some things but totally unaware of others. He hardly ever noticed Vince, Aoife, Vince Jr or Lucy, even if they spoke to him. Their names seemed to come as a surprise to him sometimes.

And she recalled nearly every detail of their childhood, how he was so different to other children. While boys of his age picked their noses, he picked his private thoughts, internalising everything.

Through her bedroom window, she used to watch his mum, Hanna Kelly, bring him outdoors at mornings to feed pigeons. Hanna was tall, as Wilf would grow to be, and always casually elegant in flared skirts or slacks, pink or yellow sweaters. She would slide into her Renault 4 car and drive it a space forward, to create a special place for Wilf to attract his birds by tossing out cornflakes.

Pigeons flew down from Felicia's side of the street. She realised they were perched on her roof. They were waiting above her head for Wilf. He must have fed generations of them over the years.

She thought of the time he'd jumped on a bin while she was being rolled in it around the Green. She'd heard a clatter on the metal and her friends laughing. When she crawled out, she saw Wilf lying on his face and began laughing too. His nose was buried in grass and his trousers stuck up in neat folds ironed by Hanna.

But he was a little too still. She went over to help him.

He was looking at something over her shoulder, but there was grass on his face, so she licked her fingers and wiped it off.

'I'll take you home, Wilf,' she heard herself whispering, before glowering at her friends and telling them to 'piss off'.

92

AT school, she saw how his eyes began to light up when he noticed her.

She couldn't remember when he began to respond to her chatter. But once he started, he said anything that came into his mind. Sometimes he'd embarrassed her.

'You left your fly open, plonker,' she said once when he came out of the school bathrooms. She zipped it up for him.

'They're looking at you,' he said.

When she turned around, other schoolkids were gliding in and between groups, glancing her way, and sniggering.

'Let them,' she said, her face reddening.

But she also found out that Wilf was a marvel at school stuff. She began to take advantage of his talent, always sitting beside him in school tests.

'Accommodation?' she'd whisper.

'CC, MM,' he'd whisper back.

She chose the right spelling on her test paper.

They did what kids did. Bonded.

Her mother and Hanna never really hit it off and kept a distance. Her mother was a staunch Irish Catholic from Fermanagh, and quickly figured out that Wilf Kelly was an illegitimate child.

'A little bastard boy,' she said, sniffily, 'but I suppose they all look cute at that age, to their mothers, anyway.'

So, the women didn't speak if they passed on the street.

It was Wilf himself who settled the hostility. He met Felicia and her mother on one of his wanderings as they walked home from Mr Gupta's shop with bags. Wilf got one of his determined, curious looks.

'Why did your dad leave your mum?' he asked abruptly, striding up to Felicia.

In the moments while they were taken aback, he added,

'My mum says he went off with a younger woman.'

Felicia's mother's eyes seemed to bulge, but Felicia defused it all by saying, 'Wilf, help us with our bags.'

Wilf took both of her mother's bags and one of Felicia's and carried them.

Later, Felicia's mother paid a discreet visit to Hanna Kelly. They drank wine and parted on good terms. Afterwards, Hanna made a banoffee cake and waved Wilf into the kitchen to help with the preparations.

'Wilf, love,' she said, as she took biscuits from the cupboard to crush. 'Never talk about Mrs O'Dwyer's husband. Wilf? Wilf, are you listening?'

'Never talk about Mrs O'Dwyer's husband,' repeated Wilf.

93

FELICIA never married.

She had a string of boyfriends, especially when she went through a peroxide phase, bleaching her hair blond and wearing demi-cut brassieres. When Madonna adopted the same style, she quipped, 'My copyright, bitch.'

Vince's father was a sensuous soft-spoken man with Jamaican parents. She met him at Notting Hill Carnival, where he was dancing bare-chested in pantaloon trousers on a float. He hoisted her up to dance alongside him. They were together for two years.

She loved to rest her hand on his smooth skin, between his torso and biceps, and pull it and herself along his body all the way to his ankle. She curved her hand around it.

Beauty was a man's ankle. They were overjoyed when she fell pregnant. And, whether illegitimate or not, her mother was deliriously happy to have a grandchild, and never called Wilf a bastard again.

During the first Iraq war, her lover burst into patriotism and abruptly joined the army on a four-year contract, quitting his job in London Underground.

'What about Vince?' carped Felicia. 'When'll he see his father?'

'It's not like I'll forget about him,' he replied in his soft voice. 'Sweetie, I have to do this.'

'Go your own fucking way,' said Felicia.

They never fell out but drifted apart. He was there for Vince, whenever possible, in and out of army duty, and he later taught his son to drive. He was married now and lived with a wife and newer kids in Camberwell. Back with London Underground. Standing on platforms advising people through a hand device to 'let passengers off first, please'. It paid well but, to his regret, he realised his long army stint meant he had missed opportunities to train as a Tube driver, which paid far more.

94

DURING her peroxide phase, men seemed to fall over themselves to get at Felicia. She watched their faces when they first saw baby Vince, and none of them lasted long, except the one who became Aoife's father.

He was a schoolteacher from Dublin. He taught in the same Chamberlayne Road school that she and Wilf had attended. They met in a pub and liked each other instantly.

The first time he saw baby Vince, he grinned and said, 'Jaysus, the head on that thing!'

'The bodies catch up,' said Felicia. 'All babies have big heads.'

'Yeah, and boys grow up with them,' he agreed.

After watching how he reacted to Vince, Felicia then made sure that he met Wilf.

'Hrymmphh,' said Wilf.

'Back at yeh, bud,' drawled the Dubliner.

She could tell Wilf liked him, or at least felt unthreatened.

They were together for six years. When Aoife was born, he attended her birth. Unknown to everyone, he smuggled a bottle of champagne into the delivery room. As if by magic, he produced it at the moment the umbilical cord was cut and popped the cork. The medics were too busy to stop him.

'I thought you were wearing a sock in your crotch,' Felicia said weakly to him, when he handed her the bottle. She took one gulp and handed it to a medic.

'I'm breastfeeding,' she explained.

95

WHILE life was happening to Felicia, Wilf grew older but changed very little.

Jobless and with his mum dead, he had no income, but found new routines to live by. He ignored and then threw away post, until one day Felicia noticed, and insisted that he let her read his letters. Soon, she was talking to him about bills. He grew irritable and said nothing, until finally she hit on a little girl wile to get through to him, 'Wilf, they're hassling me, now. They think I'm your stepmother or something. Can you help me deal with them?'

'Okay.'

Felicia arranged for a social worker to visit, but he wouldn't answer the door. Finally, she escorted him on trips to several offices, where people of various job titles spoke to him. He was repetitiously asked two questions:

'Are you okay, Mr Kelly?'

'Do you understand, Mr Kelly?

He always answered 'yes'. In reality, people didn't understand him.

By this means Felicia helped him get his life sorted out, so that he could be left alone. He was placed on disability benefit and sent a Giro cheque in the post every two weeks. Being Wilf, he brought the letter over to Felicia, who opened it, and then handed him his cheque.

Time became more his than ever.

His house gradually began to show clutter. The first thing he ever brought home was a painting he found leaning against a garden wall. It was a familiar one, called 'The Card Players', by Paul Cezanne. He had seen it in the book by Phaidon.

His mum's TV still worked. He sat watching it often. He liked to stay up late to watch Open University programmes. He loved it when graphs or charts or maps suddenly appeared on screen. But most programmes were unwatchable, especially foreign-language ones with subtitles. He turned those off and walked around his home, before turning the TV on again to see if it was still foreign.

Felicia once asked him, 'What do you do at nights?'

'Tutankhamen,' he said, thinking of one of last night's OU programmes, about Egypt.

'Do you know, you're leaving your lights on all night?'

'It's my house.'

It took a few days for Felicia to find a way to deal with this.

'Wilf, your lights are keeping me awake. Can you turn them off please?'

'Okay.'

It was another little girl wile that worked, reducing his energy costs.

But stubborn Wilf took the TV from the living room and carried it up to the back bedroom, where he slept.

He could watch it all night, with the door closed and the light on, where Felicia couldn't see the glow. If a foreign programme started, he could turn off the TV, and edge around his home in the dark, feeling his way.

96

THE one thing his life lacked was books. He missed them, but without his mum, they seemed as if missing a purpose. Books were a shared sensation, initially between a writer and reader but, in Wilf's experience, much better as a ménage-à-trois.

'Okay,' his mum used to say regularly, taking a book away from him, 'What did you think of it? Wilf, are you listening?'

'Santiago likes lions more than fishes.'

'Why do you think that?'

'Kills fishes but dreams about lions.'

His mum nodded, knowing that Wilf had noticed things in Hemingway's *Old Man and the Sea* that others didn't. In this way, they talked about many books, in their own private club. But after her death he couldn't read them anymore.

The world felt bad without her.

A rack of newspapers stood outside Mr Gupta's shop. Starved of reading, he started to stand there in the mornings after feeding pigeons. He read all the headlines and parts of the front pages.

Mr Gupta came out one day but, as Wilf was turning to rush away, gestured him to stay with his finger.

Mr Gupta was Indian and often seemed reserved, but then would suddenly decide something and burst into movement.

'Your mother liked the *Guardian*. Do you want one?'

Wilf thought about it, looking at the abundance of newspapers. Finally, he made a choice.

'I'll read the *Times*.'

His mum had once said, '*The Times* is the voice of the British establishment.' He was curious to know what an established Britain sounded like.

Mr Gupta scooped a *Times* from the rack, but instead of giving it to Wilf, led him into the shop. He reached over the counter for a scissors and then clipped out the *Times* masthead. He gave Wilf the newspaper. Wilf just stood there, staring at the scissors.

'Why?' he asked.

'Ah! Newspaper companies. If papers we can't sell, they won't take them to the rubbish anymore. I have to get rid of them. I cut out the top to show the ones we can't sell. For rebate.'

Wilf felt disturbed by this information, though he understood it was because Mr Gupta was good with accounts and paperwork, like his mum had been. Mr Gupta had told Felicia of plans to expand his shop by becoming a franchise of Spar, and installing a freezer section.

But as he walked home to read the *Times*, he thought about how desecrating page one of a newspaper meant that on page two, there were things impossible to read fully. When he got home, he pulled open the paper. Part of an article was gone. He read what was left.

> '... spring burst. My favourite ash is in the cemetery I often write about in this column. It has a deep-carved boot-print bark, riddled with age. If you pull down the brushes of leaves now, in May, you catch a faint scent. Only if you crush a leaf against your nose, can you feel a real sensation of ash.
>
> Ray Houghton © 1990

Wilf knew that ash tree. It was in the cemetery. It stood over the grave of someone called Ebenezer Windsor, who died in 1903. He discovered newspapers are full of discoveries.

97

FELICIA was still nursing Aoife in her early weeks when her mother died suddenly. It was a heart attack. 'Fermanagh women have the heart of a cow', her mother used to proclaim, to impress upon Felicia the importance of heritage, 'too big.' She had her heart attack on the Number 18 bus, trying to struggle up to the top deck while the bus was jolting from a stop.

Felicia, in her grief, waited for Wilf to come out to feed pigeons, then went over to share the news. Wilf said nothing. He spread a few extra cornflakes.

'Do you want to come to her funeral?' she asked.

He said nothing again but went inside his house. Before he shut his door fully, he opened it again and said, 'No thanks.'

Felicia understood. Her news had sent him back into Hanna's death. She felt touched. If he really hadn't cared, he would have said, 'Good day to you, Felicia.'

She went to the funeral with Aoife's father beside her, his arm around her shoulder. He held Aoife in a papoose on his stomach, over his dark suit, while Vince, who was a rebel now, kept trying to yank his hand out of hers on the other side.

Later, she discussed the future with Aoife's father. He said they could live together, as a family. He didn't mention marriage, but left it unspoken.

She decided against marriage, unspoken. Unspoken still, he seemed hurt.

'Why can't we carry on as we are?' asked Felicia.

It was the start of their break-up. Years later, he got married to a pregnant Birmingham woman on his fortieth birthday. Aoife was a bridesmaid. Felicia, in a reversal of normal roles, was best man, handed over the ring at his ceremony, and made a funny speech.

98

BOTH her and Wilf had become orphans.

In the years that passed, imperceptibly, Wilf's gatepost began to tilt. Nanometre by nanometre, it bowed towards the ground, pulling away from mortar. Piece by piece, like Pisa by Pisa, it leaned, making Wilf's home the tree streets landmark.

Felicia saw less and less of Aoife's father. But he stayed fair with money and came around to whisk Aoife off to Madame Tussauds, multiplexes, London Zoo, even Alton Towers. He took Vince too. It wasn't an afterthought. Vince was never an afterthought.

Felicia felt she worked thousands of jobs while her children were growing up, cleaning, pouring, typing, organising, standing at a Portobello Market stall, occasionally signing on as unemployed but doing a little cash-in-hand work. She often thought, while filling in forms that asked for her 'occupation', she'd like to write the most genuine of London job-titles, 'ducking and diving.'

99

IN his private world, Wilf one day climbed over a fallen piece of wall at the back of the cemetery. The canal ran just alongside. He watched water ripples, moor hens and ducks. He stared up through tree leaves at the big sky, then at the barges moored on the far bank. It was peaceful. He heard a hammering sound.

He looked up and spotted a woodpecker. Clinging to a high tree trunk, banging its beak against a spot, a little red-headed bird fought to get at a grub.

Wilf remembered pictures of birds he'd seen in books, or when his mum pointed at a living one to name it, though sometimes his eye wasn't quick enough and the bird was gone. But his mum never spotted a woodpecker in all the times they'd walked in the cemetery, though she held him still sometimes, watching a goldfinch or snapped her fingers if she saw magpies.

'Those yokes are thieves,' she said.

The woodpecker was the first best thing he'd seen since she died. He wished she was here, so he could point at it. Curiously, he found his eyes seeping tears, warm salt tears, which they had rarely ever done before.

He finally cried for her. It took a long time, while a swan drifted across the canal, to look at him from one of its eyes.

100

HE saw many new things after she died.

He felt there were two ways of seeing. One is to see things out there, like the woodpecker, or a swan, or a blue damselfly in the cemetery. His mum sometimes prevented him seeing things in that way, like when he went to explore a crashed car on the side of Elm Road, with a wheel tilted in. She pulled him back.

'That's an insurance case. We don't want to be involved with that.'

'We don't want to be involved with that,' responded Wilf.

But alone if he saw a damaged car, he forgot everything she said. He moved his fingers over the dents. The car was like a wounded artwork.

101

THE other way of seeing is inside yourself.

Inside yourself was like seeing sensations, bytes of knowledge, intuitions. His mum often tried to draw him away from those, too. Because he spent too much of his time in there.

'Wilf? Wilf?' she said, again and again. 'Are you listening, love?'

He was generally elsewhere. But heard her words.

'Wilf, are you listening?'

He turned his eyes to her so she would know he was listening, though listening felt like in-and-out osmosis, undertaken against his will.

One evening, when he was a small boy, she sashayed into the living room like a fashion model, wearing her old fox-fur wrap across her shoulders, deliberately catching his eye. Then she sat by him on the sofa where he watched TV and entwined the pelt around their legs.

Wilf didn't know it at the time, but this was another of Hanna's many efforts to get through to her child, to help him connect.

'Feel it,' she said, stroking the fur. 'Doesn't fox-fur feel lovely.'

Wilf felt it.

'What does it feel like?

'Fox,' said Wilf.

'Do you want a choice? Wilf, Wilf, do you want a choice?

'What choice?' he asked, visibly thinking about it.

'We can watch TV or I tell you this fox's story.'

'Fox,' he said.

His mum turned off the TV.

'This boyo,' she said, tapping the fox's head, 'scared my grandmammy half to death, your grandmother's mother.'

'Great,' said Wilf.

'Great grandmother. That's right. Good, Wilf.'

'Peig Kelly.'

'Yes, her name was Peig,' she said, pleased. 'When did I tell you that?'

She could see Wilf focussing.

'On her birthday.'

'Yes. On all her birthdays. You're a listening little yoke.'

'I'm some sort of yoke,' said Wilf.

'You're my yoke!'

His mum gave him a squeeze, as she often did.

'Now, feel the fur. Doesn't it feel soft?'

Wilf felt the fox-fur and looked at her.

'Look at the teeth,' she said, lifting its head. 'Aren't they sharp?'

He felt the sharp varnished teeth in the fox's mouth.

'Now, when my grandmother was a young woman in Waterford, her father and our fathers before her had a farm. She went out one morning to the chicken coop to collect the eggs. She had to kneel down to get inside. Do you know why she had to kneel?'

Wilf looked at her.

'She had to kneel because it was a chicken coop. Wilf, why did she have to kneel at the chicken coop?'

She saw a little light in his eyes, his mind's light.

'Coops don't need to be tall. Chickens can't fly.'

'That's right, they can't. Chicken coops are like houses with little doors. My grandmother had to kneel in to find the eggs. But she got a terrible fright. This fox was inside.'

She tapped the fox's head.

'This boyo here,' reinforced his mum.

Wilf looked at the fox.

'It'd got into the coop. It jumped at her, but just when she thought it would bite her, it squeezed out past her shoulder and got away in the fields.'

'It was alive,' said Wilf, meaning that he understood the fox pelt had once been as active as a London Zoo animal.

'Hens, chickens I mean, got killed. Hens are chickens but . . .'

Wilf stared elsewhere and she knew not to explain further.

'Wilf, are you listening?'

'The fox killed the chickens.'

'This one did,' she said, tapping its head. She left him a few seconds to peer at it some more, in the way he did.

'My grandmother was in shock. The family were poor enough, you know? They lost half the hens and all the eggs. And the income. But the shock of its big teeth!'

He put his fingers on the teeth again and looked in the fox's eyes.

'Now, all the men in the district liked Peig. They couldn't get enough of her. She was the best-looking woman this side of the Suir River.'

'Suir?'

'It's a river. Like the Thames, but fish can live in it.'

'Do they bite?' asked Wilf.

'Irish fish bite bait, not boys,' said his mum. 'So, all the men in the countryside tried to kill this fox. This one here.'

She tapped the fox's head.

'They went out into the fields, standing out all night, with shotguns. Shots were ripping off all over Waterford. Cows and sheep were getting slaughtered by friendly fire. Finally, one of the men shot this fox.'

She tapped the fox's head.

Wilf tapped it too.

'It didn't get away,' he said.

'Peig recognised it. It was the one in the coop. Do you know how she knew, Wilf?'

He looked away from her.

'Wilf? Are you listening?'

Wilf seemed to re-focus.

'You know how she knew? You see this mark here on its face? Put your finger on it.'

He put his finger over a little dark mark on its face fur.

'She saw that mark when it jumped at her. She knew it was the same fox.'

'It didn't get away,' he repeated.

'The man who shot it is my grandfather. Your great grandfather. She married him.'

'We eat chickens too,' observed Wilf independently, and not at all curious about marriages.

But this was the first time Hanna really felt Wilf was making a joined-up effort to engage. It was a seminal moment.

102

FELICIA inherited a matriarchal streak from her mother, who was like a momma elephant among docile London herds. Somehow, authority made for a happy home, and she went along with it. After her mother died, she became the matriarch.

Vince and Aoife went along with it in their turn, despite rebellious phases. They grew into mostly considerate adults. Sometimes, if she was troubled by Wilf refusing to sign a form or change his clothes, Vince said: 'Ma, forget about him a while.'

Aoife added, 'He's as right as fucking shite, Ma,' one of the turns of phrase she'd picked up from her Dublin father.

'Do you have to swear like that, Aoife?' said Felicia.

Her kids kept her feet on the ground, kept her thinking practically. As her years passed, her concerns about Wilf zoned around persuasion, signatures, application forms and little victories to win the state benefits he needed. Meanwhile, her real children unresentfully looked after themselves and made their own mistakes.

Vince and Aoife became party animals. She didn't like their choice of lovers, of which there always seemed new ones. Boyfriends and girlfriends swung through the house like rotisserie dishes.

Vince brought home an angry girl from Harlesden who stuck her tongue out and put ecstasy pills on it. She soon became a pregnant angry girl. Felicia helped her through the birth. One day a few weeks later, she put the baby boy in the girl's arms, and studied her face as she fed Vince Jr. She realised the girl was still immature. The experience of birth hadn't helped her grow up. But she decided not to intervene.

At the weekend, she walked into the kitchen to find Vince feeding his child alone from a bottle.

The girl from Harlesden was gone. Neither Vince nor she said anything.

Aoife's child was born just over a year afterwards. The father had crew-cut hair, rode a Suzuki motorbike, and wanted to learn to fly helicopters. He slept in and out of the house during Aoife's pregnancy and brought in bottles of Captain Morgan rum. Felicia began pouring these down the sink. She found Aoife in the kitchen one morning nursing her new-born child, her face heavily bruised.

'Where is he?' asked Felicia sharply.

'Gone,' said Aoife. 'I kneed him in both nuts.'

Felicia felt relieved.

'Hell-lllooo Lucy,' she said, twiddling the baby's chins.

Somehow, the O'Dwyer house grew happy, matriarchal or not.

103

YEARS passed. Wilf grew more refractory, ruder, difficult to persuade, more resilient to wiles.

He stopped signing forms, even when she desperately pleaded they were for his benefit. His mum never liked forms. 'Gateways to debt,' she described them.

Felicia couldn't sign anything on his behalf. She had no power of attorney, and she wouldn't humiliate him by calling in more social workers or shrinks to certify his vulnerability and force him into being a ward of court.

Wilf's life began getting harder. He lost his electricity first.

He noticed that neither his lights nor his TV switched on one night. Felicia warned him this would happen.

'What'll you do when it does?' she'd asked.

He responded to it by changing his routines. He went downstairs in the dark, into the kitchen. There, he lit the gas burners on the stovetop and basked in its bluish but steady light. He found a copy of the *Daily Mirror* and began to read.

Then, he lost the gas too.

But he remembered that in St. Aubert's Church, there was a candle stand with rows of tea light candles. He always liked their glow.

Boxes of tea lights were sold at the supermarket on the Grove. He began to buy them when he had enough money. He liked the way wax pooled into a liquid cavity as the flame burnt and evaporated. He learnt to read with ease in low light.

Frequently on Fridays, the Vicar of St. Aubert now gave him bags of church tea lights and talked to him about a divine triangle – God, taking care of oneself, God caring for all. They were disparate ideas. But the Vicar was a centre-of-balance man, so Wilf once said to him, 'God is the middle.'

'Exactly right,' said the Vicar. 'God is the centre of everything.'

Felicia, in her turn, often sighed but accepted Wilf for who he was. She tried more and more to intermesh with his routines.

Only once did she fly off the handle with him. She found him searching in a bin and emptying out dirty bags to put into his pocket.

'Don't ever do that,' she stormed, 'you're not a bum.'

'I need bags,' said Wilf.

'For God's sake. It'll get you into trouble. It's illegal.'

'Is it?'

'Yes.'

'I need bags.'

'You can have mine when I come back from shopping.'

'Okay,' said Wilf.

She knew better than to ask what he needed the bags for.

104

Now, he was dead. Life had switched off suddenly, like his electricity and gas.

Earlier, when she'd arrived back from Wembley Police Station, her front door seemed to click shut like a loud clock tock behind her.

He was dead but seemed swimming with life in her mind. She leaned against the door a little woozily.

She realised her home was silent. She listened.

She was alone. Vince and Aoife and the kids were gone. Why?

It took her a few moments to realise why: they were considerate. They were giving her space to process her grief, do what she wanted or needed to do. She could rage around her house, wailing, hitting walls, if she liked, get herself drunk, hurt herself, mourn, cry, collapse on the floor. They'd pick up the pieces when they came home.

Felica prowled for a while in the empty rooms, not yet knowing what to feel. She was too exhausted for pain. She ran a bath and poured in some bubble concoction belonging to Aoife.

She removed all her clothes and stretched in the warm water.
He was dead.

She thought about her future without him. What would he say, if he were standing outside the door, waiting to use the bathroom? Probably, 'get new routines.' He wouldn't want her sniffly or needy or sorry for herself.

And what would happen now that he was all over the news?

As she lay later with her face curled into the pillow, trying to sleep, she thought she heard sounds outside, at times in the night. But unknown to her, she had fallen asleep. Vince, Aoife and the kids had crept back into the house to watch over her.

PART 3
FIRESTORM

105

WHEN Felicia woke in the morning to a media-mad world, the idea of 'news' would connect itself in her mind to the poet, Kevin Curran.

When Kevin first moved into the area, he grew matey with Vince. He started dropping by, sharing cans of Guinness and the odd joint. Kevin was sociable and talkative, though he had a bit of a dreary voice and his moustache looked like a bad case of alopecia.

Felicia's curiosity was piqued one day when he started droning about the four stages of a media firestorm.

The storm hits you first like a physical storm, he claimed – faces, phones, lens, questions, sympathy, assumption, doubt, hatred. A commentary wave cuts in and the storm blows itself into panel questions, Op-Eds and chat shows. It ebbs into freelancers and press interns, hoping for a leftover fix. Cynicism and archival hope linger last, where, if you make news again, your old news is dragged out.

He said the worst time was when the second wave was fading. You had a tiny space and felt more depressed than ever in your life.

Later, Vince looked up "Kevin Curran, Irish poet" on the web, and found out he'd once been in a lot of trouble. He showed his mother a short video of Kevin's head being pushed down into a police car in New York. The report under was headlined, 'Suspect with Terrorist Links in Custody.'

'There's more to that boy than rhymes,' she observed.

Plain nosey, she poked details from him about his arrest, but could get little about the so-called murder he'd been investigated for.

'Police cock up,' he explained. 'It was actually suicide by heart attack.'

According to the news report, he had been found in a lift with the dead body of an American business tycoon. The lift doors had opened in a crowded lobby, unveiling Kevin apparently trying to resuscitate or complete the assassination of a man on the lift floor.

Felicia thought it might not be a smart idea to get nosey about his "terrorist" links. But she got nosey anyway.

'My dad,' he droned. 'He was mixed up with the IRA. He smuggled weapons and explosives. Allegedly. Never convicted. He's from Belfast. My mam was a manic depressive from Sligo. I got a job in New York to get the fuck away.'

It took Vince quite a lot of online research to confirm that Kevin's father was - allegedly - a mastermind behind arms supplies to the terrorist organisation. There were no photos, except one of him with a parka hood pulled tightly around his face, in dark glasses, pallbearing a coffin at an IRA funeral.

'Judged by the sins of the father,' commented Felicia.

106

Now, on the morning after Wilf's death, she climbed out of bed, dressed slowly and went downstairs, where she hoped to drink tea and eat a slice of toast, while talking intimately to Vince and Aoife, to start the grieving process.

Instead, she was hit by a media firestorm that would unfold exactly as Kevin described.

The first she knew about it was a call on her Nokia.

'Felicia O'Dwyer? I'm with the *Daily* . . .'

'How'd you get this number?' she interrupted. But didn't wait for the answer, just ended the call.

She found Vince and Aoife sitting quietly in the living room, waiting for her. Vince Jr and Lucy were beside Vince, sharing some sort of game on his tablet.

'What's going on?' asked Felicia, hearing noise filtering in from the street outside.

'Don't look out the window,' said Vince. 'There's a fucking army out there. We're under siege.'

'TV cameras and all,' added Aoife. 'We disconnected the doorbell. Didn't you hear them ring it earlier? They were knocking as well.'

'No, no, I was . . . totally unconscious.'

'I phoned the five-o,' said Vince. 'They've sent some boots.'

'What'll we do?' wailed Aoife.

'Oh, Jesus, I can't think of anything without a cup of tea,' said Felicia.

She went into the kitchen and put on the kettle. While it was boiling, she thought it over. She decided to ring Ray, who wrote for the *Times*, to get his advice on how to deal with the press pack.

'I'm sorry about Brian,' were Ray's first words on answering. 'I hope you're not upset, Felicia. We're all sorry for your loss.'

'Brian? The one with Kanga Girl?'

'Yes, I . . . think he's trying to get ahead. He's young. His report in the *Times*, it's sort of, not balanced.'

'Oh, shit,' said Felicia. 'Is it trouble?'

'I'd say so, yes.'

Felicia ended the call and yelled: 'Vince, I need to read something in the *Times*.'

Vince, in his lazy way, rooted on his phone, by-passed the *Times*' pay firewall, and found the newspaper's report of the Yew Road Siege, written by Brian Tomkins, photographs: Kanoni Makame.

She hated scrolling through its small print, but grew more engrossed and horrified as she read on.

Big Don had destroyed her. The reporter had lapped up every word he'd said during the siege, when the big man had approached through the crowd.

Don claimed that Wilf had exposed himself to children. He had often been worried about Wilf's strange behaviour, and alerted parents. He always told children if they saw Wilf: take photos. He was afraid of cameras.

Felicia O'Dwyer, he added, was a bully who always confronted anyone who expressed concerns. She'd defended him for years. And tonight – while the police were trying to arrest him for murder – she was organising a riot. She had led all these people out on false pretences.

Inset in the article was a wobbly video of Wilf taken, obviously, by a child. It showed him peering over and then hunching with a lot of bags, then scarpering up Yew Road. It must have been a shopping day. The video looked to have been recorded from the playground. It was silent, but Felicia could imagine the words 'Smelly Kelly' ringing out after him.

Don never talked to kids or parents. He lied. But it was remarkable that journalists had dug up a smart video so quickly.

There was more. Big Don also claimed that Felicia had made money out of Wilf.

107

THAT was true.

Felicia had worked as Wilf's formal carer for a few years. Back then, social services were allowed to use common sense and discretionary funds when protecting vulnerable people. Wilf would never let a stranger near him, but Felicia was like family. So, she managed to get a part-time wage. She kept his lights and heat running and managed his money. It was ducking & diving, a way of life in London.

After a change of government, there was a change of policy, and she was told that to continue, she needed to gain qualifications. She refused, out of pride, and ended up without pay while Wilf simply dropped off the radar.

She wanted to use her savings to pay his bills, but Wilf said, 'Good day to you, Felicia.' She'd never do anything without his consent. He deserved dignity. 'I'd better take over your laundry from now on, Wilf,' she'd said, feeling defeat.

In a dramatic climax, the *Times*' article finally revealed that Big Don, "an almost broken man", had a final revelation.

108

BIG Don claimed that Felicia had tried to evict him.

She was voluntary Chair of a local Housing Cooperative, which usually involved her sitting in meetings and signing end-of-year accounts. The Co-op owned houses around the tree streets, including Big Don's, on Elm Road. He'd lived in it with his mother since a boy. After her death, almost immediately after her burial, Felicia had tried to turn him out.

That was almost true. She'd visited Don not long after the funeral and asked him to consider moving into a smaller place. Obviously, a big mistake.

She'd offered him a renovated one-bedroom flat on Beech Road. Applied a bit of repetitive pressure. He no longer needed so many rooms. There was a refugee family in need of a house.

She realised now it was utterly insensitive. She'd turned the big man into an enemy, and before long, he started his 'unfit-to-live' campaign against Wilf.

On top of the shock and pain of Wilf's death, this now felt like she was being kicked while helpless on a floor.

109

SHE had a long history with Big Don. When they were teenagers, he had fallen madly in love with her.

As a youth, he was the opposite of what he was now. A tongue-tied boy with strange oyster-like eyes. If they passed in the street, he said 'Hi' and swept his oysters away. He was secretive, so she hadn't realised the direction his big eyes were secretly tending.

He played football for his school on the Willesden side of the tree streets. The Willesden schoolboys always beat the Chamberlayne schoolboys, and Big Don was their defensive rock.

A talent scout for Chelsea football club noticed him.

He was invited in for a trial, playing a in football match amongst other triallists and Chelsea youth club apprentices. His team won 3-2. But for the two goals conceded, he was at fault, too slow in turning to stop fast boys running past him. They would have scored more but he started barging and tripping. He almost broke a kid's ankle.

He failed the trial.

Afterwards, during a buffet, each of the triallists were spoken to individually by a legendary Chelsea player, with a shake of the hand and an autograph. He signed the shirt Big Don played in, with a crayon.

Months later, it was Felicia's sixteenth birthday. Her staunch Fermanagh mother said to her, 'You're old enough for a party now, Felly.'

So, Felicia was allowed to organise her own party. 'Just don't go wild,' warned her mother.

An excited Felicia invited her friends to invite theirs and repeat the message. A lot of people were guaranteed to show up.

On the big day, her mother took a taxi to stay overnight with a relative in Colindale. As she left, she said, 'I want to find the house in exactly the same state as I left it. You're the woman now.'

It was a banging party, absolutely noise central. It spilled out into the garden, where Hanna Kelly was sitting at the rose plant with Wilf, who didn't want to mix. Felicia knew better than to bother him, and Hanna kept her arm draped on him, and talked to him constantly.

Felicia loved him for being here. She knew how hard it was for him.

She had her first experience of marijuana, doing a thing called 'blowback' with a fast-talking boy from Elm Road. She knew what boys really wanted, and she always challenged them to show it, so she could refuse.

She received a lot of cards and presents. Big Don, who arrived late, gave her a soft-feeling droopy present in gift-wrap paper that she recognised from Mr Gupta's shop.

She unwrapped it and found a Chelsea football jersey. She unfolded it. It was a number 5 shirt, the number Big Don always played in. It had a signature in crayon above the number.

'Does that say Chopper Harris?'

'It's genuine,' said Don.

Felicia noticed the hope in his face and found herself cringing internally. She froze between cackles of giggles and wanting to be kind to the boy who gave her a gift.

She sensed that Don sensed the same thing.

She always suspected he never forgave her for that.

He wasn't her type. Poor old Don. He was disappointed in love years later too, with a girl from Sheffield.

110

SHE decided she would have to phone Don. Even before dealing with the media, she should bury the hatchet with the big guy. Though it was hard for her to forgive what he said about Wilf. That was pig-ignorance.

She calmed herself in the living room, standing in her certain way with her thumb and middle finger on her eyelids, her family waiting for her to speak.

'I'd like to see what's going on outside,' she said.

Vince tactfully disentangled the two small children from his tablet, and replaced it with his smartphone, which let them take photos of each other. He went to the window, slid the tablet around the side of the curtain, and recorded the scene, with a slow sweep of his wrist.

He pulled it back inside and showed Felicia the video.

There really was an army of media. Their numbers spilled in an arc. There were news cameras on tripods, more on shoulders.

To her surprise, Padma and Eric were standing guard at her gate. They prevented anyone ringing the doorbell.

'Those two?' she said.

'Do you know Padma's a qualified childminder?' said Vince, 'and Eric's sister is an MP for Peckham.'

'Jesus, Vince, you're as nosey as I am.'

The video also showed that a police forensic team were in Wilf's house, a tent shrouding its door. A rectangle of blue tape had been unwound, calibrated so that cars could still edge by and neighbours gain access to the adjacent houses. A lot of uniforms were still around.

By this point, she also saw cameras pointing at Vince's tablet, recording him recording them.

'I'm going to have a fucking conniption,' she said. 'Vince, can you do anything about those . . . bastards out there?'

'Give it a try, I guess,' said Vince, nonchalantly. 'It's about time the Bros had a challenge. Don't worry, Ma.'

Vince was a handsome grown man now, his nose identical to his father's. But he always had a wicked little play on his lips that she reckoned came from her.

On his side, Vince never told her about seeing Wilf on the doorstep, and firmly intended never to do so. It wouldn't have prevented him dying.

111

VINCE tapped on his tablet and messaged all his Bros while Felicia peeled away into the kitchen to phone Big Don.

Within five minutes, Vince had gotten every one of his friends onto a video call, linking in Paulie Carson too, whom he reckoned by now had enough soul to be a real Bro. Paulie's twin sister, Susan, photobombed the call and sat in also, her face near his.

They weren't the only twins on the call – the Kellett twins were here too, younger than Vince, but chilled guys.

'Know you got *papoozi* outside your house?' said Ade Kellett, the senior by two hours.

'No shit, Sherlock,' said Vince. 'What are we going to do about it?'

'We?' asked Malaki Kellett, the younger.

'C'mon, Mal. Ma's cut up about Worzel. She's helped you out a few times, hasn't she, when you needed someone to talk to.'

'Your ma's a legend,' said Ade. 'Hands up anyone who'd swing for Felicia.'

All the Bros' hands went up on screens. After a while, Susan put hers up too, shyly beside Paulie's.

'So, what can we do, then?' asked Malaki. 'Play us the script.'

'I don't know,' said Vince.

Susan put her hand up again.

'Do you know Eileen, the Texan? I was talking to her last night, and she doesn't like the press. She said, do you know what journalists are afraid of? Being asked questions.'

'Ahhh . . .' said the Bros, almost collectively having the same thought.

They agreed a plan quite quickly after that. The Bros met up at the house of their newest Bro, Paulie Carson, in 24 Oak Road, and after firming up their tactics set out to silence the media.

They did it by mingling, standing close and asking questions.

The Kellett twins were first to roam down Yew Road, as if taking a stroll. They were actual actors. Both had got into a school of dramatic arts, and Malaki had featured in a Lucozade ad. They were fraternal twins. Malaki was bulky and gangsta, wearing a gold chain on his neck; Ade was smaller but could act hard.

They walked up close to a journalist, who said, 'Hi.'
Malaki touched him lightly. 'Got any money?'
'Got money, blud?'
'Bro needs money. Got any money?'
'Gimme some money, blud.' Ade touched the journalist.
'Look in your pockets.'
'How much you got?'
'What's in your pockets?'
'Show me your phone, blud.' He touched.
'Show him your phone.'
'You TikToking?'
'What's on your phone?'
'You TikToking? You Instagramming?' touching.

They could keep this up for long minutes, unsmiling. The touching was the torture. Ade was worse. You saw in his eyes that he knew you had something to hide. He was improv. Malaki was script.

Meanwhile, the other Bros drifted singly into the crowd of media and, friendlier than the Kelletts, poured out questions, the stupider the better. Gradually, they worked reporters into wider spaces between each other, and no matter what was said back to them, they could say more.

Susan attached herself to a woman reporter. She gave her a lot of good advice about the area, especially never to use the Brazilian hair stylist by the diner (they'd once snipped someone's ear lobe). Her brother decided to be creepy, also zoning in on women. He said nothing, just stared in their face. If they turned away, he stood close behind them, so that they could hear him breathing.

A camera on a tripod began to topple inexplicably before its owner grabbed it upright.

The police refused to get involved. Padma and Eric pointed out that nobody was committing an offence, while the paparazzi were disturbing the peace.

Before long, the media began pulling to a safe distance down Yew Road. The Bros hung around Felicia's gate, smoking, talking, and teasing the cops. Padma and Eric stood aside to allow Malaki to knock on the door.

Vince looked out from behind the curtain and Malaki gave him a thumbs up.

Vince was surprised by how easy that had been. He felt a little disappointed that none of the paps were visibly doing a story about the intervention. It felt like they didn't know what to do about being caught off-guard, by this type of people.

Felicia came out of the kitchen.

'What's going on out there?'

Vince drew the main curtain aside and lifted the net curtain. The Bros outside waved at Felicia, pointed at her, and one put his finger to his head and pretended to blow his brains out, which she took to mean that the paparazzi felt like committing suicide.

'I see Susan's here,' she said, waving back. 'She needs to get out more, she's too pale.'

'She still has a crush on Norris,' said Aoife, facetiously.

'What do women see in that fucker?'

Aoife said nothing, because she had once slept with Norris, and her mother knew she had slept with him. Her mother, never one to pull punches, had said – 'Aoife, your problem is you like rough-house boys.' She was right. But, at least, *Susan* didn't know she'd slept with Norris. That would hurt the poor girl.

'OK. I have an announcement,' said Felicia.

Her family looked at her. Little Lucy took a cheeky photo with her uncle's phone, and gave her a 'gotcha' grin.

'I've made a deal with Big Don. We're moving into his house on Elm Road. He's moving in here. We'll have an extra room.'

'What the fuck?' said Aoife. 'He'll mess up his place for spite.'

'This house is still too big for him,' said Vince.

Felicia waited patiently while their complaints dispersed, and the idea of an extra room registered.

She felt sorry for the refugee family she'd wanted to help. They would end up wedged in a renovated one-bedroom flat. But as she'd spoken to Don, a feeling came to her that she no longer wanted to live opposite Wilf's house, to watch it being auctioned on the open market, with strangers moving in.

Vince, in his mind, was suddenly planning Venetian blinds and a set of shelves for his vinyl collection.

Aoife hoped they could do up the attic, so the kids or her mum could sleep up there. Or her.

"Now, that lot,' said Felicia, nodding her head to mean the media outside. 'They'll camp out a few days, won't they? How'll we do our shopping? Aoife, you?'

'Naw,' said Vince. 'I'll ask Malaki. He can loop around to Spar.'

'So, that's it then. We'll wait it out.'

'Did you hear that, Vince Jr.?' said Vince. 'That means no more wetting the bed.'

'Leave him alone,' said Felicia. 'Vince Jr, what's wrong, love?'

Vince Jr had begun to seem moody and had shoved Lucy a few times. He gave a lonely look to the adults, especially his grandmother.

'Is Uncle Worzel really gone?' he asked.

'Yes, he's gone, love. He's never coming back.'

112

Felicia had no time to cry for Wilf. No time to mourn or plan his funeral. No time even to wonder how on earth a fox came to be in his house. A beautiful, beautiful fox, trying to defend him.

The media firestorm continued to engulf her family.

To them, the fox was a sign of a degraded man. TV broadcasted a news report with film shot inside Wilf's home. It showed piles of tangled junk, boxes, newspapers, clothes with what seemed to be bloodstains. A black off-licence bag had a meaty mess inside it that looked like liver.

'For fuck's sake, Ma,' said Aoife. 'We shouldn't have left him in that state. We should have tried to get in his house.'

Felicia felt herself inhaling deeply, hurt. But she stared down her daughter. 'No, we shouldn't.'

'Sorry, Ma,' said Aoife, curling her legs on the sofa. 'He was just fucking stubborn.'

'He was.'

'Look at this one,' said Vince, who was scrolling on his phone. '"SQUALOR IN PSYCHO HOUSE." Headline.'

He flashed a news screen at them.

'Vince,' said Aoife. 'Why do you have to show it to Ma for?'

'Sorry, Ma,' said Vince.

'Wilf,' said Felicia firmly, 'didn't kill Luca. He couldn't hurt anyone, except himself.'

'I know, Ma, but how are we going to prove that?'

'I haven't a fucking clue,' said Felicia.

113

THE firestorm kept burning in exactly the way Kevin Curran described.

News was repeated over and over again. On TV, she grew used to seeing the clip of Wilf, peering at the playground and rushing with his bags up Yew Road. She kept her phone turned off, to prevent press intrusion, but knew she must also be missing calls from a lot of people she loved. She sent texts to Vince and Aoife's fathers, saying, 'Don't call me.' She knew that her kids had already spoken to them, to keep them away, to protect their own families and new children.

She received replies from both.

'Wilf didn't do it, did he?' wrote Vince's father.

'I ♥ Wilf,' texted the Dubliner, who now lived in Birmingham.

Felicia scrolled through her contacts list, pausing at names of people she wished she could call. Professor Emma. Maureen. Ana. Beardy Callum. Friends she'd known for a long time. But she couldn't drag them into more trouble.

114

VINCE'S Bros were a small resistance clan, but the media were bigger. They had a twenty-four-hour cycle and could afford to rotate staff. They drew around her house again, while the Bros dwindled. Some bored journalists began shouting questions at her window.

A sharp rap on the door alerted them that Padma and Eric had granted someone access. Vince took it on himself to answer, and inside came DI Solomon and Ana, in uniform.

Ana strode to Felicia who got up to hug her. Felicia waved her hand at the DI and drew him into the hug too.

'It's a shitstorm,' said Ana. 'In Czech, we call this Průseru, but English has more words for shit.'

'I'm really sorry, Felicia,' said Solomon. 'This was all my fault. I started it all.'

'I made it worse,' said Felicia.

'Officially,' said Solomon, 'there's a reason we're here. If you feel unsafe, we can move you and your family. We've put arrangements in place.'

'Where to?'

'A secure location in Luton.'

'Vince, Aoife,' asked Felicia. 'Do you want to bring the kids to Luton?'

'Luton,' said Lucy, thinking it sounded like her name.

'They can all go and shite,' said Aoife, sounding exactly like her father. 'They won't drive me out of my home.'

'Inspector,' said Vince seriously to the police officer. 'Nobody is going to hurt my mother. They'll go through me first.'

'I don't mean it like that. We've put protection around your house. You are totally safe.'

'But we see death threats,' said Ana. 'On social media. Even on your account too.'

'My WHAT?'

'Ma,' said Aoife, 'we didn't want to tell you this, did we, Vince? You've got a Facebook page now.'

She pulled out her private smartphone and showed its screen to her mother. Felicia saw a profile photo of herself on a bright Facebook page, lumpy in old slacks. It was one taken while she was outside Wilf's house, turning with her chins folding, glaring as the *Times'* reporter called out her name. She looked wretched.

'I'll strangle that bitch with her kanga,' she swore.

'Yeah, but Ma,' said Aoife, 'look at what people are saying. Look at this one.'

Felicia read a Facebook post saying: THIS POST HAS BEEN REMOVED FOR VIOLATING OUR COMMUNITY STANDARDS.

'Oh, the moderators blocked it,' said Aoife. 'But it was like, saying, I'll cut that paedo-loving slut into strips and feed them to a fucking dog.'

'Aoife, not in front of the kids!' said Felicia, surprised to find that she was sounding suddenly like her Fermanagh mother.

'Ma, I don't give a shite,' said Aoife. 'No-one's going to drive us out of our home.'

You're turning into a matriarchal little bitch, thought her mum, proud as hell.

'Do you need any food, or clothes?' asked DI Solomon.

'We've made arrangements for all that,' said Vince.

The DI offered his fist to Vince, and Vince fisted back.

'Steve,' said Felicia, remembering Solomon's first name. 'Thanks. I can't remember the name of your boy?'

'Davy.'

'Bring him to play with my grandkids. That's Vince Jr, and that's Lucy.'

'Luton,' said Lucy.

'Da,' said Vince Jr, 'Lucy is calling herself Luton. She's stupid.'

'Davy's too young,' said the DI.

'Kids connect. Trust me,' said Felicia.

Solomon decided to bring Davy to Felicia's house one day, when the chaos died down. He found himself wanting to give Felicia another hug, so he did.

The murder investigation was over, anyway. Kelly had killed Luca Vignal. There were no other leads.

115

THE only bright spark in Felicia's life now was Malaki Kellett. He swung by from Spar with their groceries. His twin, Ade, sometimes followed, but it seemed, with Ade, he was always studying people, to improvise their characters.

When Malaki walked up Yew Road, the paparazzi withdrew on each side warily. He looked dangerous. He really was a good actor. He was in constant phone contact with Vince, so knew what to buy, what to bring, and how to throw a silencing glance if a reporter badgered him with a question.

Felicia always watched Malaki's legs and ankles. He was such a beautiful man.

Eileen the Texan texted to offer free legal advice, but when Felicia accepted, the advice was, 'There's nothing we can do right now. You might think about an interview, though.'

'No,' replied Felicia, frankly repelled by the idea of speaking to the people camping outside her home.

On TV, Wilf and the siege became talking points for news pundits, daytime chat shows, and stand-up comedians. Press columnists wrote savagely or sanctimoniously, convinced by now that Wilf was a brutal killer, and Felicia, at best, a fool. Questions on care-in-the-community were raised in Parliament.

The *Metro* published a statement on its front-page saying Wilf Kelly was never authorised to deliver newspapers on its behalf.

Felicia began to feel more depressed than ever in her life.

By the weekend, the police had released a statement saying they were looking for no other suspects in connection with Luca Vignal's murder.

Only one thing was remarkable. Nobody on the tree streets gave interviews. Now even Don was declining to talk.

116

IN fact, tree streets people found it impossible to believe that Wilf had murdered Luca the Frenchman. Both were well-known, though discovering that Luca had a wealthy background was a shock.

Luca and Wilf were like secret marginal competitors in the neighbourhood eccentricity stakes. Luca brought his shopping home in a wheelbarrow. But Wilf always edged it in overall estimation.

Just about everyone, from kids to grandparents, had got a 'Hrymmphh', at some time. He often responded with it if you just glanced at him. Abrupt, never frightening. Many people just remembered him standing in the street as they passed, studying something that caught his eye.

There were always groundswells of protection towards him, some even felt a little affection, no matter how rude he got. Everyone had a personal reason to like him.

Susan Carson had a soft spot for Wilf from teenhood, precisely because of his rudeness.

When she was fifteen, her twin Paulie was playing a football match in the ball court on Yew Road. She was on the side-line watching every challenge and felt like trying to control her twin's body each time he got the ball.

The odd guy called Worzel was also staring and swaying with the action, outside the high wire fence surrounding the court. She noticed him because he stood there a long time. He was like a seasoned spectator watching his favourite team.

Paulie tried a long shot at goal. The ball soared over the wire fence and bounced around the road behind Wilf.

Wilf – or Worzel, as she called him then – astonished her. He raced after the ball and followed it bouncing around the road.

When he grabbed it in his hands, she knew what he was intending to do.

He was going to try to kick it over the wire fence back to the boys. But she knew he'd miss it, or sky it, or knee it, and be laughed at. He'd do everything wrong.

'Worzel, hold it for me,' she shouted, sprinting towards him.

He heard her and stared and then dropped the ball to the ground and walked away. It should have felt insulting, but he had done the right thing. He'd saved himself from mockery.

117

THE three Toms became involved with Wilf as a form of retirement therapy.

As well as having the same name, all three were, by coincidence, the oldest men alive on Yew Road.

Strangely also, all three arrived in the same year. The first, Mayo Tom and his wife, Maureen, bought Number 43 outright, after selling a house in New Cross Gate. They moved from south to north London so that Maureen could take a senior nursing job in nearby Paddington. She was younger than her husband. He was retired and had an income from houses in Mayo, but she needed a home near the hospital.

She arranged viewings, in Kilburn and nearby, but it was when Tom emerged after looking around the empty rooms of 43 Yew Road, observing the tree street, with taller trees on the Green at the end, and tallest trees over the graveyard wall beyond, that she knew he wanted to live out his days here.

'This'll suit us,' he said, in his unassuming way.

They bought their new home.

The Englishman called Tom moved in next door, Number 41, a house owned by a charitable Housing Association. As a veteran soldier, he'd been shifted around many places, often with women, ultimately with a wife, who died in their flat in Bow. He felt he couldn't live there anymore. He put in an application to move. Soldiers like him, who took bullets for their country, had earned respect. The Association supported veterans.

On being allotted upstairs at Number 41, he complained in writing that, because of the old bullet wound in his hip, he couldn't go up and down stairs every day.

The Association ignored his letter in the best sense. They never went through with plans to divide the house and put in a second tenant. They left 41 to Tom alone.

Bulfast Tom, the youngest and biggest of the three, moved in last. He still wore his hair long around his neck, streaked in grey. He was tall enough to carry his belly well. He rented Number 45 from an old friend, who charged him a friend's rent. He moved in with his Filipina wife, Maja.

He explained to his new neighbours, 'I was in the merchant navy. I had wives in all ports.'

Maja said, 'But me last, uh?'

'You only,' said Bulfast Tom, drooping his arm over her. 'I never married but your little arse.'

'He's lying,' said Maja. 'I'm wife number three.'

'Men,' said Maureen. 'If they can't lie, they can't open their mouth.'

'Ah come on, now, Maureen,' said Mayo Tom. 'Was that not a lovely declaration of love?'

'It might be,' she conceded.

English Tom, meanwhile, was gawping at Maja's legs.

The three Toms and two wives made normal lives. Maureen was the busiest, rushing off to the hospital at all hours, on call. The Toms, retired, got into routines, and watched life through their windows.

Outside their three homes, Wilf, a close friend of Felicia O'Dwyer, who lived down the street, walked past, at various times of day. In the mornings, he carried newspapers. They often saw him.

'Pathetic,' voiced Bulfast Tom on one get-together evening, while all of them drank whiskey. 'Pathetic human being. We should do something for him.'

'What?'

Then one of them had an idea. They thought of a way to brighten up Wilf's drab life a little.

118

PROFESSOR Emma fell in love with Wilf.

After her awful accident, when she'd walked in front of a speeding motorbike on Harrow Road, she woke up to see soft night lights in a hospital ward. She noticed a bag of liquid, hanging from a pole. She became aware of someone leaning over her.

'Emma?' said a nurse.

All Emma remembered of her accident was one instant. She

and the biker saw each other and simultaneously she tried to guess which way he would swerve while he tried to guess which way she would jump.

In retrospect, when she thought about those days, her historical intellect persuaded her that she owed her rapid recovery to politics. A social-minded government was in power. In a rehabilitation centre, physios worked on her upper body strength and taught her tricks to lift herself on and off a wheelchair. She learnt again how to use a bathroom – embarrassing at first, being escorted. She loved swimming in the physio pool, where she imagined herself like a new type of mermaid, dragging long trailing fins.

Meanwhile, the workings of social money edged in to help pay builders to adapt her house for disability use, and her job was kept open.

If she had been injured today, the story would have been different. Britain had changed. Hostility had laid a dead clamp on society. Trauma jabs were aimed at people the nation previously cared about: the disabled, moneyless, too old, too young, too divergent, depressed, foreign or born foreign who lived entire conscious lives in the UK. There was less money, less staff, more legal restrictions, more bureaucracy. Universities disposed of staff without a second thought. She was glad she'd met the bike in 2008 and not today.

She wasn't a political woman, but history was nine-tenths politics and needed to be interpreted through cold facts. The world had got worse, not better.

On her first few nights home, after being dropped off by a National Health Service minibus with its inbuilt lift for wheelchairs, she felt isolated. Her loneliest moment was seeing a ramp instead of a step outside her door at 50 Yew Road.

She busied herself learning to re-adapt to her house, going up and down the stairs on a chairlift, getting in and out of bed, dropping coins on the floor and picking them up, using a reacher to put books on shelves and take them down, finessing her manoeuvres in the bathroom and new kitchen unit. She hurt her fingers often by hitting them against edges of things as she wheeled around.

Her garden was slabbed over, easy to wheel around in circles. She used it for exercise and balance.

She read a lot. She tried not to feel so alone.

She phoned a few of her old lovers, who'd tumbled in and out of her life. She phoned academic friends and caught up with their research. Neighbours called around. She was happy to see anyone at all.

All three Toms from across the road crowded in with their two wives, chattering, tidying things up and admiring her adapted kitchen unit. Maureen put her number in quick-dial on Emma's phone, in case she had a fall. Maja, the Filipina, said, 'If you don't fall, she does nothing. Lazy, uh? I iron your clothes for you to go back to work.'

'And if you ever need anything done around the house,' boomed Bulfast Tom, 'call Tom.'

'Got it,' said Emma.

'You still have a real woman's body, Emma,' said English Tom, who was gawping at her. 'Smasher.'

'Got it,' repeated Emma.

'Tom doesn't mean to be crude,' intervened Mayo Tom.

'I know,' she said, flourishing a smile.

'You should hear what he says to the able-bodied,' commented Maureen.

'I know how to respect people in wheelchairs,' said English Tom. 'Don't lean over, they're not deaf. That's the rule, isn't it, Emma?'

'Exactly, Tom. I'm flattered. But I don't fancy you. And I haven't heard the word 'smasher' since the 1970s.'

She did feel a frisson, though. She was still recognisably a woman. And men were still reassuringly stupid.

When the Toms and wives left, they took her laundry with them.

Felicia O'Dwyer and her son Vince visited next, bringing a hot Irish bacon meal, and a surprisingly good malbec wine from Argentina.

'Where did you find this?' asked Professor Emma.

'You won't believe me.'

'Try.'

'Jim Lyon. He heard about your accident and gave it to me for you.'

'The butcher?'

'He used to be an item with Wilf's mum. She taught him about wine.'

'There's more to meat than meets the eye,' said Emma.

Vince did the plate work, laying the table in her bay window alcove, setting out plates and cutlery, slicing the bacon and spooning out potatoes and cabbage onto their plates. It was he who poured their glasses of wine.

As they departed, Vince leant over and gave her a warm hug and kiss on her cheek. He left a small bag of marijuana by her side in the wheelchair.

But still she felt lonely and desolate.

Early at mornings, she glided downstairs to read up on her specialist topics, especially Eleanor of Aquitaine. Eleanor was a Queen of France who lived in medieval times but felt as modern as her. While medieval men with real minds debated abstract problems of universals, Eleanor set up a practical Court of Love. Real lovers came and squabbled out differences. She judged twenty-one known cases before male wars interrupted. Some of today's scholars argued the Court never truly existed. Emma was convinced it must have done in some medieval form not yet understood.

The proof was modern women, setting different priorities to argue with men about.

One morning, Professor Emma sat tired at her alcove table, reading about Eleanor. She felt pain everywhere. Sensations in her legs were like digital code playing out in nerves. But she was determined to go back to lecturing soon.

Suddenly she heard a sound at her front door. Her letterbox lifted and a squished newspaper was pushed in slowly through it, until finally gravity pulled it to the floor. It splayed out with the name *Metro* on its front cover.

'Wilf?' thought Emma.

She rolled back her chair, turned and wheeled to the door. Opening it was still awkward, but she made it out and rolled down her ramp into the street.

It was deserted, from here to the far end.

'Wilf,' she called, but nobody answered.

She felt a warm feeling, like love.

119

BEARDY Callum had a strange dream, a few days after Wilf's death.

In it, he saw Wilf walking along Yew Road, hunched over with bags. Behind him a big red fox trotted, so closely its nose narrowly avoided being kicked by Wilf's heels. When he got to the end of Yew Road, Wilf realised he'd overshot his house. He turned back. Towards mid-street, he was lost. He didn't know which house was his.

The fox trotted straight to Callum's door, in his point of view.

He saw it sit down, looking up expectantly like a dog anticipating a treat. Wilf approached too.

Callum saw his own hand opening the door. In his dream, he was living in a house on Yew Road, blocks from his flat on Ash Road.

As he opened the door, the fox trotted in as if at home.

Wilf stopped at the doorstep, and offered him a copy of this morning's *Metro*, which, for some reason, had a picture of Callum himself on the front page, under a headline stating, 'Fake Ladies for Wilf.' When he looked down, he realised he was wearing a mini skirt. When he looked up, a photographer was taking his photo.

Wilf stayed holding out his *Metro*.

Beardy Callum woke up. His bedroom was in its usual configuration, piles of books and magazines around the floor. Reassuringly, his loved map of Cuba was still pinned in its frame on the wall, and a signed photo of Castro.

It felt like in the dream Wilf was sending him a message about acceptance. It felt like he was endorsing Callum's right to live in his own way.

120

To Ana the Czech, Wilf was like a 'Welcome to Britain' meme with an image of an English eccentric.

She'd spent what amounted to her life savings to move into the tree streets and he was one of the first people she met.

She had just graduated as a Metropolitan Police officer. Until now, she'd shared a room with another Prague girl, in a stinky house in East London. She lived there all through her years working at Pizza Express before becoming a police trainee.

Days after signing her contract, becoming a real cop, guaranteeing more pay, she emptied her bank account and paid a deposit on a one-bedroom garden rental on Yew Road, close to her posting in Kilburn Police Station, on its cheaper side. With the remainder of her savings, she went to Car Giant and bought the cheapest used car in stock.

It was a Fiat Cinquecento. Its engine was sound, but no matter how many times she put it through the car wash, its paintwork still looked like someone had mauled it with sandpaper.

Nevertheless, she loved her new car and new job, and her new flat, and the way high trees loomed at the end of Yew Road beyond a wall. She learned that the tree streets were named after types of tree planted in the overgrown cemetery. It was more like a jungle than a cemetery.

Living in London filled her with pride and anxiety. She tried to absorb the English mindset. She took a drive to see the famed city of Oxford, which turned out to have less soul than Prague. On another weekend she drove to Bedford, a prettier town where a friend of hers lived by the River Ouse. It was an experience of a more real England, where middle-aged women sold homemade jam outside the library, to raise money for charity, and determined young men practised speed-rowing in crews on the straight stretch of the Ouse.

Ana and her friend took bread and pastry outdoors one morning to feed the river geese, cruising in orange-beaked meanderings on the water.

A big swan was resting on the bank nearby and ran at her as she began throwing crumbs. It grabbed her by the sleeve and she dropped all her bread, drawing a swarm of birds onto the bank.

'Kokot,' she hissed at the swan in Czech. She thought of aiming a kick but then remembered her British police training.

'Common assault, but no actual bodily harm,' she whispered to herself, mentally charging the swan.

Her car also proved a godsent during her time as an undercover prostitute, catching kerb crawlers. She could leave her house with a coat covering her work clothes – micro skirts and cut-away tops or a catsuit. She drove to her post, put in her hours, drove to the station to file her reports, and drove home. No need to change clothes in locker rooms, no fuss, nobody staring at her on public transport. She could also wash her own clothes, rather than put them through police laundry services where, she felt sure, prostitute garments were not welcome, as they might entangle in dryers with commissioners' tunics. An image like that might end up on social media.

One morning as she emerged from home early, on a non-prostitution day, she saw a strange man interfering with her car.

He was badly dressed and her trained eye picked out the curious details. He had layers of clothes and a splitting belt. The head of a toy dinosaur bobbed out of his anorak pocket, surrounded by a hedge of what looked like bags. Clearly a crazy man.

'What you think you're doing?' she demanded, expecting him to rush away.

'Hrymmphh,' said the man holding his ground.

He was taller than she first thought, glancing at her and shifting his face away then back.

She looked at the *Metro* he had stuffed under her windscreen wiper.

'Did you put newspaper there yesterday too?' she asked.

'Are you a Pole?' demanded the man, in his turn.

'No, Czech,' said Ana.

The answer seemed to puzzle him (unknown to her, Wilf had never met a Czech before).

'Do you read news?' he asked.

'Yee . . . ss,' she said, not yet sure how to handle him.

'I can leave the *Metro* at your house. Number 25.'

'Ooo . . . kay,' said Ana slowly, realising that – for him – this was what the English called "a thing". His thing. In Czechia, they'd term it an obsession. But obsessives in England were called 'eccentric', and always had 'a thing'.

'Listen,' she said, 'don't put papers on cars, okay? That's anti-social behaviour.'

'Is reading the news anti-social where you come from?' asked the man.

Ana found herself grinning internally. Not so long ago, the answer to that might have been 'yes', and maybe might still be.

'OK, bring me the paper. But you might get hurt if some bastard catch you touch his car.'

The man seemed to sway for a moment on his feet, forward and back.

'Good day to you,' he said, and walked off abruptly. Cutting her off seemed so natural to him, it didn't offend her. She eased the *Metro* from underneath her wiper.

She had only for a split-second thought of arresting him, which was within her powers even while wearing plain clothes.

121

THE Kellet twins, Ade and Malaki, had changed Wilf's life forever.

When they were kids, they were always getting up to no good. They were clamberers from a small size who figured out how to stand on each other's shoulders to pull down the Benin tribal mask on their living room wall.

They were fridge raiders who opened every container and left stuff they didn't like on the floor. They always had to tidy up afterwards but did it again.

They were cat hunters in the back garden. Soon all life forms avoided them. Their mother, however, noticed that no matter how wildly they chased, or what they dug up, they never once knocked over her flowerpots. They knew her flowers were her pride and joy.

She always said, 'Those two egg each other on.' Though born in Nigeria, she sounded like a private schoolgirl of 1950s England who had gone on a summer safari and had a holiday romance with an African park ranger. But she also knew how to pinch a boy's ear like a true Lagos dame. If her husband looked on disapprovingly, she said, 'Dis boy, E restrict my airflow.'

'Give your mother her space,' said their father.

The boys were natural leaders and, as they grew into school life, formed a little posse around them. They thought up dare tests for new members, who had to balance upright on the spiked school railings without impaling themselves, while the posse counted to ten, at their own pace. If a boy or girl couldn't pass the test, they couldn't join.

Nobody died. The posse grew quite large.

Ade was always the one coming up with new ideas and tests. He thought up the ultimate test. Applicants had to stand upright on the playground swing with their hands above their head, while the posse counted aloud to ten.

Nobody succeeded in standing for a full ten. Most didn't make it to two. It made the Kellett posse more exclusive.

'Posse need name,' said Ade. 'Fam gang. If you get in with we, you fam.'

Malaki loved the name. Most gangs called themselves after districts, like the E13s, or the Harlesden Cribs, or the Harrow Rude Boys.

'Fam Gang,' he intoned resonantly.

A cheeky Fam Gang member challenged Ade to prove he himself could stand on the swing. Ade did it with ease, hands above his head, for a full ten count. It was simple to figure out the trick. He swore everyone to secrecy.

Ade and Malaki also spent a lot of time alone, staking out mini territories, thinking up things to do. They loved the canal with its long towpath from Little Venice to Scrubs Lane, which had lots of hiding places in the bushes. Ade had a pile of ideas: they could stuff stones down the chimneys of the barges moored on the canal and watch inhabitants rush out in smoky panic, they could lead a trail of food for ducks into the bushes and throw a coat over one, they could knock over one of the annoying towpath cyclists into the canal and run off with the bike.

'Yo, they're on our turf, bruv,' said Ade. 'We need smart moves.'

But when Malaki, a more focused boy, stepped out towards a cyclist, Ade held his sleeve.

'Yeh, but if he can't swim,' he said.

Malaki looked at his older brother, as if seeing him in a new way. Ade had a neat English nose like their father, but tall Malaki had prouder nostrils and realised he could look down around them, while Ade looked up.

He finally understood that all their lives Ade had come up with the ideas, while he came up with the execution. Ade was improv, Malaki was script.

But they balanced each other out.

One day the Fam Gang saw the weirdo called Worzel walking

with a lot of heavy bags past the ball court. They were standing around, talking excitedly about a film they all watched on TV last night. It was about a crazy dead freak brought back to life if you said his name three times.

'Fam. Let's bring the bro to life,' said Ade suddenly. 'C'mon.'

Ade ran in front of the gang. They all caught up with Wilf and surrounded him. Ade slid-danced in front and said, waving his arms:

'Beetlejuice. Beetlejuice. Beetlejuice.'

'Beetlejuice. Beetlejuice. Beetlejuice,' the gang chanted.

Wilf said nothing, kept his head down and kept walking steadily.

"We're done, Fam,' said Malaki, standing still and waving them back. 'Leave him alone.'

They all stopped and allowed Wilf to go home.

Over the years, Malaki and Ade grew into smart creatives whose acting and mimicry talents got them into drama school. Wilf, for the rest of his life, had an extra nickname.

As adults, both of them were painfully aware that he turned away or crossed the road if he saw either of them. Ade one day called as Wilf turned away.

'Wilf, man, I'm sorry.'

122

SUPINE Mario regarded Wilf as a saviour.

He came slowly awake one morning on his bench, after sensational experiences with e's, coke, crystal, Jack Daniels and temazepam.

The willow tree by the ball court was leaning its usual shelves of leaves above his head. The ball court was empty, and the London sky was striving to find its purest blue in too many clouds. He saw the odd bird called Worzel leaning over him, in a raggy, stained shirt.

'Worz . . . ?'

He realised Wilf's hands were on his body, on his neck, a finger pressing on a pulse point. He understood what was happening. Worzel thought he might be dying and wanted to help him to stay alive.

''S okay, Wilfie,' he said.

'Good day to you,' said Wilf, taking his hands off and walking away.

123

NORRIS'S mum liked Wilf because he noticed her.

She was a frail thinning woman whose ventures outdoors were long-distance if Norris was in prison, but shorter when he was free.

As she grew older, she loved to tend flowers and little green growths. She planted a line of herbs on her front garden wall in pots that Norris had given her, swearing he bought them in Sainsburys Garden Centre.

She was watering the line of herbs one day when Wilf, walking down the street, held his hand under her spraying can.

'No,' he said.

'Don't need water,' he added. 'Let them grow first. They learn to cope on their own.'

Wilf, big, tall, reached over the wall and cupped his fingers gently around her knee. She felt the warmth of his skin.

'Is it always sore?' he asked.

'Every day.'

'Keep walking,' he said, his eyes turning away from hers. 'Move it.'

She felt almost privileged. Wilf hardly ever touched people.

124

EVEN Norris respected Wilf, after a fashion.
Norris stole a car one night. He rammed his elbow through the driver-side window and opened its door from the inside. He was out of his mind, drinking wildly, coking, cracking, e'ing, fucking. But there were no women around tonight, not even Susan.

He drove the car suicidally fast. When he got to corners, he remembered how to use the wheel counter-intuitively to steer into the hard lurch.

He raced around and around the tree streets.

He wasn't asleep, but in a dawn trance, when he crashed into the metal railing protecting the children's playground. It slowed him down so that when the car hit the wire perimeter, the airbag blew out in his face, and he could fall asleep.

Tight fingers on his shoulder woke him up. He heard police sirens. He was dragged out of the car by a strong hand. It was Worzel.

'The bushes,' said Wilf, pointing at the vegetation around the playground. Norris ran to them to hide.

125

ISLAND Garth was a big Wilf fan.
Wilf knew what it was like to live without money. Garth's wife, whom he loved dearly despite her dreariness, was right to handle all the household income, leaving him broke. He would just spend it all otherwise.

One evening, Manchester United were playing in the Champions League Final. Garth was watching his beautiful team stride out onto a big screen, while he stood outside the huge windows of the Masons Arms pub.

Wilf was on one of his routine walks and circulated behind him. Garth said nothing, because he knew if he said, 'Wilf, are you okay?', Wilf would walk away.

Wilf came up beside him.

'Who are they playing?' he demanded.

'Chelsea,' said Island Garth.

Wilf abruptly started digging into the pockets of his jacket and trousers. He found a few notes and coins and put them into Island Garth's hand, not looking at him.

'Go in,' he said and walked away.

126

UNKNOWN to both, Big Don had been there that evening, watching from the Green. He saw Wilf give the money to Island Garth and Garth going inside. He went over to the pub and looked through the windows. Island Garth had bought a beer and his eyes were now glued to the screen. Don too watched, as the United left-back skipped past a Chelsea player's challenge.

Don turned around and looked up at the Green across the road with its playground and ball court on the far side. Wilf had disappeared.

He thought about himself.

He had been a triallist with Chelsea. If he'd got through, he wouldn't be playing football at his age, but he might be on the coaching staff, on the sidelines at the final.

He felt suddenly astonished by Wilf. He never thought the defective man could behave in this way.

But then he felt a devastating loneliness, standing on a pavement outside a pub. He thought about his ex-girlfriend, from Sheffield, her hazel eyes through prescription glasses, looking up at him, so unique. He decided to walk out onto the road in front of traffic and kill himself.

He went out onto Harrow Road, spread his arms and closed his eyes. There was no traffic. He dropped his arms and opened his eyes again. Nothing appeared except food delivery cyclists who swerved around him on scooters, delivering pizzas or curried food with bags of poppadums, to households that had phoned or ordered online.

He couldn't even kill himself.

He realised all of Britain was indoors watching Manchester United play Chelsea in the Champions League Cup Final.

He went home to watch the final too.

When he got inside, in Elm Road, his mother was watching TV.

'Mum,' he said. 'Can I change the channel?'

'You always want to change the channel,' she complained.

Years later, after she was dead, and his home was threatened, Big Don tried to run after Wilf in the street, to ask him to ask Felicia to let him keep his house, even though at the same time he was collecting signatures against him. Unlike Wilf, he could cohabit with disparate ideas.

127

RAY who wrote for the *Times* sometimes – secretively – included Wilf in his columns. He called Wilf, 'the Shadow Man'.

> 'I was walking silently on the dirt track to the coppice, when I saw the Shadow Man with his back to me. He was startled still, transfixed, watching something. I couldn't see what he was watching. Suddenly a parakeet shot out in a swerve of

green from the direction of his intense gaze and arrowed above my head . . .'

Ray Houghton © 2004

When he was desperate to finalise the number of words to fill his column, he frequently drew on Wilf.

'. . . As I stood in the dwindling sun, declining through the leaves of Wiltshire, I imagined myself as if I were the Shadow Man, alone, watching, waiting.'

Ray Houghton © 2016

Whenever he mentioned the Shadow Man in his columns, next morning he would wait for Wilf to approach with the *Metro*, then open his door and slip him a bit of money.

128

LUCA the Frenchman had always been pleased to see Wilf. Wilf reminded him that life was often funny.

Luca was an obsessive collector, and often went to auctions or brought home still useful items found on the streets. One day, he found an iron girder in a rubbish skip and decided it was valuable enough to store in his shed to find a later use for it. He hoisted and dragged it out under his arm. He was strong.

He dragged it a good distance along Beech Road, before letting it clang to the ground, and sitting on it for a breather. He saw Wilf approaching on his *Metro* round. Wilf diverted before Luca's house to walk up to the living Luca and hand him his morning *Metro*.

'Help me with this,' said Luca, tapping the metal.

Wilf walked around the sides of the girder, surveying it.

'Too big,' he said, and strode off. But, as if he had second thoughts, he turned back and said,

'We could put it in that skip over there.'

129

MOMENT-BY-MOMENT, Wilf grew more organically dead in Felicia's mind, through his simple act of absence. She found herself shrivelling into besieged thoughts, unable to let anything out. But finally, she was persuaded by Eileen to give a media interview.

Eileen had got through to her by phone one late evening to offer a frank Texan legal opinion: 'If you don't git in front, y'all oughta burn.'

'Can you translate that?' said Felicia.

'I've got you a TV exclusive. BBC Breakfast show. Tomorrow. I can force it to a three-minute time slot. Five – at worst. They won't ask accusatory questions. It's a good deal, Felicia.'

'No.'

'It's my advice. Start getting real. You're big news. You can't stay holed up like animals in a cage.'

Felicia began thinking it over.

'What would I say?'

'That it's not your fault. You didn't Frankenstein a monster. You tried to help all your life and that's it.'

'But Wilf didn't do it,' insisted Felicia.

'So, say so. You don't have to go into the studio. The BBC's in Manchester. You can do an interview by video.'

'I need to talk to my family first,' said Felicia.

She hung up and spoke to Vince and Aoife.

'The BBC is placid,' said Vince, warily, 'with bear traps. You'd have to watch out, Ma.'

'I can sit beside you,' offered Aoife.

So, it was agreed that Felicia would give an interview seated at home beside her supportive daughter. Vince would do the filming and steady his phone cam by putting it on a selfie stick and taping it to the back of a firm chair. He would attach his long charger lead to keep it powered.

They spoke to the obliging cops, Padma and Eric. Padma agreed to come inside during the interview and sit with the kids, with her arms around them to keep them quiet.

130

THE BBC had phoned after midnight to make everything as easy as possible.

They offered to send a London team to set up unobtrusive cameras, to help her feel comfortable. It would seem like a more personal interview, with better quality visuals.

Felicia said no. It would alert the remaining reporters outside her home before an interview even started. Those would phone others, and her family would spend the day more swamped than ever.

The BBC agreed that Vince could do the filming but persuaded her to allow a sound artist into her home to fit a microphone, so that they could at least broadcast clearly what she said.

They sent a girl who, in Felicia's eyes, looked like a humanoid sylph who slid in from the dark streets without alerting a single reporter. She had mannerisms like Aoife's, all smiles, light touch, and chatter but with a private school accent and less foul-mouthed. After fitting peanut-sized mikes to Felicia and Aoife, she purred that Felicia would look better on screen with one side of her hair pulled lightly behind her ear, showing that nice earring.

'Dead on,' said Aoife. Together, they used transparent tape to arrange Felicia's hair around her ear. Then the sylph pressed in a tiny earpiece. She did the same with Aoife, now sitting by her mother's side.

The sylph walked to the other side of the room, and whispered into a little mike in her sleeve, 'Can you hear me, ladies?'

'Loud and clear.'

'Almost done then.'

After that, it grew technological. Vince and the sylph, who seemed to find him attractive, fiddled with the selfie phone and made quiet exchanges.

'Vince, let her do her job,' said Felicia.

Vince and the sylph stepped apart and she saw on the phone screen between them a man's face suddenly appear. The face had thin hair and cherry-shaped cheeks with stubble and a warm smile.

'Felicia,' she heard it say into her earpiece, 'I'm Gary of the BBC. I'm here to help with today's interview and any questions or anything you need to know. Now your slot starts at 8.05 after the News. That's peak viewing time, it's the moment that stops commuters walking out the door.'

It was hours away.

'You might want to make a cup of coffee,' he added, 'it's going to feel like a long night.'

'Are you from Glasgow?' asked Felicia, trying to place his accent.

'Don't make me spit,' said Gary.

'You sound like someone I know from Glasgow.'

'I can see where this is going. It's the Glasgow loop. Every Scot sounds like someone we know from Glasgow.'

'Sorry.'

Felicia noticed that the sylph was leaning into Vince and saying quiet words into his ear. That boy was a fast worker.

'I'm going to get a coffee,' she said, standing up. Everyone had forgotten about why they were here: Wilf.

'It's all A-OK,' said Gary, in her earpiece. She felt reassured by his voice, that warm timbre.

'The sound, everything is perfect,' he said. 'But do you have any colourful cushions to put around your sofa?'

131

THE time came to go on air.

Aoife sat alongside her again and they gave little squeezes to each other's hands. Padma had glided in to sit down with the kids. Vince and the sylph stood behind the phone stick.

'Final screen test, Felicia, can you confirm that you see this?' said Gary in her ear.

The phone suddenly switched from Gary's face to a video of hippos, swimming in harmony underwater.

'Hippos?'

'Perfect,' said Gary. 'My little joke. We're switching to live . . . are you ready? Now . . . three, two, one, and . . .'

BBC Breakfast now appeared on screen, smartphone size. It was presented by its regular morning team of polite Phil Gaskin, who wore thin blue ties and light suits, and perky Nisha Anand, who wore auburn highlights in her hair.

'The murder of Luca Vignal has gripped the nation,' said Phil. 'The dramatic images of the Yew Road Siege were beamed around the world.'

'This morning, we're joined by one of the key insiders,' said Nisha. 'Felicia O'Dwyer, Wilf Kelly's closest friend, who has finally decided to break her silence.'

'Welcome to BBC Breakfast, Felicia,' said Phil.

'Good morning,' said Felicia.

'And beside you I believe is your daughter, Aoife?'

Aoife flushed bright red. Off-camera, Vince Jr. pointed at her, but Padma put her hand over his mouth.

'Aoife,' asked Nisha, 'did you know Wilf well?'

'Mmnnnn,' said Aoife.

After a tiny pause, Bill cut in with: 'Felicia, how did you feel when you first saw police outside Wilf Kelly's house?'

'Angry . . . ?' said Felicia, tentatively.

'Not surprised?'

'Yes, alarmed, confused, everything. I felt everything at once. Wilf was vulnerable.'

'So, you felt you had to intervene?' said Nisha. 'You started a demonstration.'

'I tried to stop Wilf being frightened.'

'Was that before or after you knew he was the suspect of a murder enquiry?'

Felicia paused. She realised these questions were being fed to Bill and Nisha on an autocue. She was talking to someone typing words to scroll in front of them.

'Wilf didn't murder anyone,' she said.

She was about to open her mouth again to claim that, if anything, Wilf himself was murdered by the inability of police to knock quietly on doors.

'We have to leave you at this point,' said Bill suddenly. 'We bring breaking news. We're going live to Downing Street, where the Prime Minister has emerged to make an unscheduled statement.'

The screen cut back to Gary's face. He gave Felicia a stoic grin and tilt of his head.

'I'm the surprise face of live TV,' he said.

'What happens now?' asked Felicia.

She waited while Gary listened to something on his earpiece.

'We stay filming, Felicia,' he said. 'The live feed will come back to you. We want to hear your side of the story.'

'No,' said Felicia.

To her own astonishment, she found herself doing something she saw often on films and TV. She made a sawing motion over her throat to tell Vince to stop the video feed.

Enough. She had said what she wanted to say.

132

EILEEN managed to get hold of her less than five minutes after the interview.

'That was short. You needed more time. Do it again?'

'No, it was a set-up, Eileen. Anything to do with the media is just attention-seeking rubbish.'

'Getting Aoife to sit in was a smart touch.'

'No, it wasn't. She's locked herself in the bathroom. She never wants to be seen again.'

'She'll get over it,'

'Eileen, I think it's a good idea if you don't talk to me for a while.'

'I . . . 'll . . . get back to you on that,' said Eileen. 'But wait and see, you'll benefit from this big time.'

She ended the call. Felicia released a huge sigh and leaned back on the cushions of her sofa.

'Vince,' she yelled. 'Is there no tea in this house?'

'I'm putting on the kettle now, Ma,' he said, still fiddling with his phone.

'No, I'll do it,' said the sylph, whom Felicia suddenly realised was still in the room.

'No, I will,' said Padma, getting up and releasing the children. Felicia realised she was still in the room too. It was as if TV had made her temporarily blind to everything else.

133

EILEEN would prove to be right.
While Padma glided in from the kitchen with a hot milky cup of tea, the sylph glided over with a mobile phone.

'The BBC measures how quickly news media change headlines

after interviews,' she said, in the casual intimacy of her posh voice, showing Felicia a news feed. '*The Daily Mail* wins every time.'

Felicia saw she was now the headline news of the *Daily Mail* website, with a photo of her and Aoife captured from the TV screen.

TRUE BELIEVER

'Wilf Kelly is not a murderer,' claimed his closest ally, Felicia O'Dwyer, in a dramatic interview on BBC Breakfast . . .

But as she read on, she found the tone of reporting towards her had softened. She was no longer the inciter of a mob, a devious fraudster, or a plain fool. She was now more of a sad and trusting woman grittily defending a man she truly did care about.

The way her daughter Aoife had held on to her hand, showed the world that Felicia was a family woman, a loving woman.

As the day wore on, she saw clips of herself repeated over and over on TV. On the evening's Channel 4 News, an eminent psychiatrist said that O'Dwyer was like a victim of Stockholm Syndrome, clinging to someone she refused to believe was capable of crime.

Outside her house, the media crews had grown even larger. But there was a different vibe about them. They no longer felt vulturous but were more like a murmuring set of concerned onlookers.

She breathed a huge sigh of relief and decided to phone Eileen to thank her. Things might be a little easier now.

134

OVER the next few days, paparazzi outside her house thinned, as news cycles began to shift elsewhere.

Then, overnight, their focus changed from Felicia back to Wilf. Suddenly, his family were in the news.

Felicia had almost forgotten he had a family.

The media had got to the bottom of his mum's secrets. *The Daily Mail* splashed it as an exclusive. Vince showed her the news feed.

'They've done a number on Wilf's mum,' he said. 'Not as bad as the *Times* did on you, though.'

The paper published secrets Wilf never knew. It spread over pages with photos, taken in various years. The oldest was of Hanna, in black-and-white. It was a childhood photo, in her Communion dress in a group, her head circled.

Even at that young age, Felicia recognised her.

135

ACCORDING to the report, Hanna Kelly had been a happy girl growing up through the 1950s and 60s in a good family in Waterford.

Felicia knew that already. She had heard Hanna's whole life story during their many years of chatting. She saw that the gist of the reporting was true. But it failed to convey just how fantastic a woman Hanna had been.

Yes, she'd had a supportive childhood, but she'd studied extra by herself and won a full scholarship to Trinity College Dublin. When the day came to leave Waterford, she was so excited she skipped onto the train forgetting to hug her family goodbye. She leaned out of the carriage window to wave to them, and her grandmother thrust her old foxfur wrap into her hands.

'Take this oul' yoke with you.'

'No, Gran,' said Hanna, but it was too late. The train pulled away, and she was left with her widowed grandmother's most precious possession, a sign of love, though Hanna had never liked it.

In Dublin, she lived for her first year on campus in the girls' dormitories. In her second year, she shared a flat with other girls who had a more free-rolling lifestyle than hers.

But Hanna had a sense of Munster pragmatism and a stellar brain. She focused on knowledge and results.

She liked to sit in on lectures on different topics. University allowed no barriers to roaming into any subject you liked. You could learn about Freud or of a unique crab caught off the Kerry coast, so big each leg drew out to the length of golf clubs. Hanna went into the Zoology department to see a specimen. She was also interested in politics.

She went to a lecture on the Irish Constitution, given by a Senator, a member of the higher chamber, the Oireachtas. It was incredibly informative. She spoke to the older man at the end about how progressive Ireland could be. Article 2 specified every person had an equal right to be part of the nation, not just every man. In the real world, it didn't feel like that yet.

The Senator had a strong investment in understanding the views of the young and invited her for a drink to hear more. He began seeing her regularly, even took her to a hotel in Kildare. They talked intensely, and he tried to argue her mind from women's lib to women edging in. He was unlike any man she had met before, until he made her pregnant. Then he stopped meeting her. The last thing he wanted was the scandal of a baby. He delegated his PA to deal with the matter.

Hanna refused to go into a Magdalene home and give her baby up for adoption. It was the 1970s now, and harder to shame girls. She carried her pregnancy through the rest of the college year, then gave birth to a son in a private ward, at the Senator's expense, in return for which the birth certificate name of the boy's father was 'unknown'.

Despite her defiance, it was still 1970s Ireland, where secrets were hard to keep. Hanna finally gave in to pressure and accepted that finishing university was impossible. And to go back to her family felt like real shame – the shame of not achieving her potential.

The Senator bought a house, sight unseen, in London, through an agency. Outside the hospital, Hanna was met by a taxi taking her and the baby to the boat-train. On arrival at London's Euston Station, with hardly any luggage and her grandmother's fox-fur wrap, she posted a goodbye letter to her family and took a taxi to an address in Yew Road, Brent.

Diligently, the Senator kept sending money. A fair allowance, indexed to inflation, taken over by his legitimate son after his death. That son had been brought up in the family trade and also became an elected politician. But the money stopped coming when Hanna died.

The paper told a more simplistic and sensational version, in which Wilf was a baby so unwanted he grew into a sociopath. They published the names of the Senator, and the son. They'd cornered the son as he came out of the Irish parliament, Dáil Éireann, and published his photo, alerting the Irish media in the process.

His office issued a statement saying, 'My accountants struck the allowances to my brother during an audit, and they were never restored. My brother never responded to communications.'

It was true. Wilf rarely took notice of letters unless the envelopes were handwritten. His mum always said, 'Print means a problem.'

But Felicia was puzzled. The politician's statement suggested that Wilf must have received letters from Ireland that he never brought over for her to read. Maybe because they were from a foreign country.

136

WILF, Hanna once said, was a son of the Oireachtas. If you slit his skin, he should bleed green. He was Ireland in all its hypocritical purity.

But as he grew up, he grew fascinated by pictures of the charge of the Light Brigade, where British horsemen ran at artillery with swords. They wore heroic red and rode white chargers. He liked photos of Spitfires and World War II aircraft, the Battle of Britain. The idea of Britain alone.

Hanna never had the heart to tell him he was born misplaced.

'If it gets inside you, nationalist crap never goes away, no matter whose side it's on,' she remarked.

'Nationalism is selfishness,' said Felicia, who often discussed politics with her.

Hanna carved out a new life, centred around her son. Occasionally, she liked the company of men. She enjoyed God squabbles with the Vicar of St. Aubert, while she had an affair with him. She loved the energy of the neighbourhood's fit new butcher, Jim Lyon, who was gorgeous. He had shoulders that could loop you like a cocoon. When he lost his finger in a cleaver accident, they secretly buried it together in the cemetery.

Hanna had been terrific fun. She always uncorked a bottle of wine when Felicia dropped by as a young adult, usually to moan about men.

'Can't keep their yokes indoors, can they?' quipped Hanna. 'Thank God.'

Now, the firestorm had moved to Ireland. The political career of Wilf's half-brother was at stake.

The whole thing made Felicia feel worse than ever. But outside her gate, she now saw just a few straggling freelancers and interns hanging around.

'Nobody even doubts that Wilf killed Luca,' she said to Vince and Aoife, who had decided after all not to spend the remainder of her life in a bathroom. 'How will we prove he's innocent?'

'Not everyone thinks he's guilty,' said Aoife.

137

MI5, MI6, secret service, detective this, detective that . . . finally the security forces had to release the poet Kevin Curran from Paddington Green police station. They returned his phone in a plastic envelope.

Kevin felt exhausted by the time he got home to his flat on Yew Road, spotting a few sore-footed hacks around the street, seeming like they wished they had chairs. Kevin guessed that cops had warned them not to lean on people's cars or sit on garden walls.

He decided not to contact Felicia or anyone else. His immediate priority was a beer. He raided his fridge, extracting beer and olives, which he consumed alongside a packet of crisps. He began feeling a lot better.

The problem with time spent in a police cell is boredom. Kevin found that it followed him on release, too. Confinement made him fonder of poetry. He'd been scribbling attempts at verse since his teens. Now, for discipline, in cells he often tried to compose new poems in his mind. He felt, if not better than earlier attempts, his words sounded more measured.

He had thought out a few new ideas and wanted to write them down. First, he caught up with the news that had passed him by while inside. The more he read on his phone about Wilf and the murder, the angrier he grew. Finally, he decided that instead of poems, he would turn to the far more effective medium of podcasts.

Kevin booted up his laptop, resisted an impulse to play a game, and pulled up his channel, set his webcam in motion. For podcasts, he sat against a wall with posters of W. B. Yeats and George Orwell behind him, personal heroes. He slipped into his Americanised voice.

'Yo y'all, and shout out global. Redemption podcast timestamp now. The poet is back.

'I've been thinking about Redemption Song by Bob Marley. I came to London because I felt this city can absorb anyone, tolerate anyone. I felt this was Redemption City. The city that freed itself from mental slavery.

'I was wrong. Not just 'cos I was thrown in jail for filmin' cops bustin' my bro, Wilf Kelly. But 'cos all the sheep in this town believe what cops accuse him of. Wilf ain't no killer. He's awesomely, sublimely, unequivocally INNOCENT. Makes me so angry, y'all. I'll stop, because I feel like ramming my fist in the screen. I'll be back.'

Kevin didn't seriously intend to ram his fist through his screen, but always felt it best to end podcasts on a melodramatic high. It helped bump up his followers' count, as did being arrested while streaming.

138

BULFAST Tom spent a lot of time thinking of Wilf. He felt guilty about making fun of him so often, though never to his face.

On the second Sunday after the siege, he spent £60 on a goose at Queens Park market. Geese were his favourite fowl. Maja, his wife, was an excellent cook and slow roasted it through the afternoon. They invited English and Mayo Toms with Maureen into their home.

Maja was – almost – a Filipina mail-order bride. Bulfast Tom negotiated with a real one but, on flying to Manila to meet, was introduced to her circle of friends, one of whom was Maja. She said, 'So she think you seksing hayop, uh? Poor girl.' He liked her right away, though hadn't a clue what she meant.

He proposed two days later and they got married in a little church during a tropical downpour. It leaked drops through the nave. She was beautiful, as she stared into his eyes unwavering, and said, 'yes.'

This evening, Maja welcomed their visitors with a tray of sherry. 'Chug,' she said and smiled.

'That means cheers,' said Bulfast Tom.

'He always says arses up and down the hatch,' said Maja. 'Make sense, uh?'

'Chug,' said Maureen. 'I think we'll keep the talk decent.'

They did. They sat around the table and Bulfast Tom carried out the juicy goose from the oven. He set it down and sharpened a carving knife on a scraper, loudly, to see if he could annoy anyone. No one rose to the bait, so he carved and said, 'Breast only unless you want a greasy bit.'

Mayo Tom lifted his plate. He liked to get things out of the way first, and then take his time to hear what people were saying.

'Can you give me a bit of both?" he asked.

'I can of course. And who'll be next?'

They all passed their plates towards him, and meanwhile Maja ran in and out with bowls of vegetables, a pot of rice and a dish with some sort of purple sauce.

'That one's for decoration,' said Bulfast Tom. 'You don't have to eat it.'

'It's Ube Halaya,' said Maja. 'Put a bit on your tongue. Sweet, uh?'

They all tipped a finger in the purple sauce and tapped it on their tongues.

'Well, I like it anyway,' said Maureen.

'So, who's going to be the rogue tonight?' asked Bulfast Tom, wiping his fingers after carving, sitting down. 'Who's going to tell guilty secrets?'

'I nominate Tom,' said Mayo Tom.

'Tom so,' said Bulfast Tom, nodding to English Tom. 'The floor to you.'

English Tom, still the old soldier, spoke of his life in brief ways – 'national service, Malaya, jungle, Aden. Got shot. Limp. Women. Wife. Her funeral.'

'Now,' he concluded.

None of it was coherent after a few drinks. But he talked about himself in his own way. Take him as he was or take a hike.

'I liked women too,' he added gawping at Maureen.

'You can stop what you're thinking now,' she said.

He gawped at Maja.

'Stop thinking her too.'

'Habit,' apologised English Tom.

'So that's Tom,' rounded up Bulfast Tom. 'Always has a way even at his age to swing life to the wife-swapping side.'

'Can I have another slice?' asked Mayo Tom, nodding to the goose.

'You can of course. I think we should open the champagne as well, as a prelude to the Bushmills.'

Maja fetched the champagne from the fridge and filled glasses.

'To Wilf,' toasted Bulfast Tom loudly. 'And his mystery fox.'

'He was a bit of a fox himself,' said Mayo Tom.

'An innocent man is what he was,' said Maureen.

They drank. Maja brought a bottle of Bushmills whiskey to the table.

'So,' said Bulfast Tom, after all the glasses were poured, 'how many years did we keep up that pantomime of hating the fuck out of each other?'

His guests quietened, thinking.

'I enjoyed it,' said English Tom.

'You enjoyed looking at my wife's arse when she bent over to pick up the *Metro*.'

'I hope we all do and always will.'

'What it was is, we had time,' said Mayo Tom. 'We're retired. Wilf needed support. We put on a show and let it get silly.'

'It was a fine thing,' said Maureen.

'Who thought it up in the first place?' asked Bulfast Tom.

'Me,' said Maja.

139

THE Carson household was subdued.

Paulie had installed spotlights in the ceiling but his twin Susan preferred a cosier vibe, so turned on just a reading lamp. She'd chosen the chintz curtain and pale blue matt paint on the wall. Paulie kept a fish tank with colourful tetras on a sideboard. He'd chosen the size of the TV screen.

He poured himself a vodka as he sat on the sofa beside her. She'd just thrown a newspaper with Wilf's half-brother's photo onto the coffee table. It also held a few schoolbooks. She was studying for a mature student 'A' level.

'Please don't drink that stuff tonight, it messes you up.'

'Just one,' said Paulie, adding in orange juice.

'Infinite series of one. You're a maths theorem alone.'

Paulie mixed the drink with his finger, which he then sucked.

'Worzel never done it,' he said, abruptly.

'Course he didn't. If a fly landed in front of him, he'd wonder how to feed it.'

'Here's to the smelly sod,' toasted Paulie, tipping his drink to his mouth.

Susan reached out and took his free hand. She flicked on the TV with the remote.

Holding hands silently the twins sat, surfing channels until they found something they both liked.

140

EARLIER that day, Supine Mario sat on his bench with the ball court at his back. He held a can of Polish beer tightly. His eyes were blind to the landing of birds and darts of squirrels. It felt like a current under air was unpicking his thoughts in whispers.

He raised his can to everyone who passed.

'Wilfie,' he yelled. 'Fuckin' innocent.'

141

BEARDY Callum was inside the Masons Arms and saw Island Garth looking in through the pub window. He gestured him inside for a drink.

'Red Stripe,' requested Garth.

Callum ordered a Red Stripe and another Cuba Libre.

Garth pinched the fabric of Callum's dress and felt it between his fingers.

'Dis thing dyed cotton?' he asked.

'I think it's got acrylic fibres,' said Callum. 'Do you like it?'

'Wife would. But she a size eight, man.'

'My hell-on-earth is changing rooms. Can't use them in women's shops. Have to buy in department stores. Not very Givenchy.'

'Mi style's charity shop plus,' said Garth.

'Plus what?'

Island Garth unbuttoned his shirt and exposed a red football jersey underneath.

'Plus Manchester United. Only football club, man.'

Beardy Callum laughed.

'I'll drink to that.'

'No, to Wilf,' said Garth. 'Only to Wilf.'

'If I could get my hands on the cunt who set him up,' said Callum, 'I'd bury him in Glasgow kisses. That means headbutts.'

They clinked glasses and took a gulp to Wilf.

Island Garth suddenly got a text. He looked at it on his phone and showed it to Callum: 'Luv ur video. Mi dad be proud. Ziggy M.'

'It's from Ziggy Marley,' he said. 'How he get mi number, man?'

142

PROFESSOR Emma invited Eileen the Texan over for dinner. It was just korma and rice from the microwave, but she'd bought a few good bottles of wine, from the Portuguese deli on Harrow Road accurately named 'Delicias'.

Eileen brought her a book, as a gift. She handed it over as she came in.

It was called, *Big Wonderful Thing*.

'I remember those,' Emma said.

'It's a best seller in Texas. I haven't read it myself.'

'I'll bear that in mind prioritising my list. What are you reading at the moment?'

'Well, strange. I'm going back to books I feel I should have read long before now.'

'The Bible?'

'Y'all askin' cos I'm Texan?'

'M'all askin' cos I wans to know.'

'What I'm reading right now,' said Eileen, 'is . . . a bottle.'

'Who wrote it?'

Eileen leaned towards a label on one the wine bottles on Emma's table.

'Quinta Do Gradil Maria Do Carmo.'

'Can we read it together?'

'Absolutely. I think it deserves to be read in depth.'

'What's it say on the back cover?'

'It's in Portuguese.' Eileen took up the bottle, parsing it through Spanish that she'd learnt at school.

'It says, 1492. The vinery was founded . . .'

'Same year Columbus went to America. Good marketing.'

'There's more.' Eileen strained over the bottle, turning it to light. 'Wild berries . . . Complex . . . I think it says at the end here, in case of Wilf Kelly, open and drink.'

'We'd better do it. 'Cos Eileen, I'm nominating you to clear his name.'

Eileen went to find a corkscrew.

143

BUT Eileen never got a chance to clear Wilf's name. On the following Thursday, someone beat her to it.

Norris's mum, accompanied by Susan Carson, led an obedient Norris to Wembley Police Station. It was a short Tube journey to Wembley Central, but a long walk to the law.

On arrival, Norris said he had an important thing to say about Luca Vignal's death, but only if his mother and girlfriend sat by him. The desk officer rang DI Solomon, who was out of the building. They waited for five minutes in the foyer, then for another half an hour in the car park where Norris could smoke, until Solomon arrived in an unmarked car with flashing lights.

In an interview room shortly afterwards, with cameras and recorders, Norris confessed that he'd attacked Luca.

That night, he couldn't sleep, he was coked out, he was looking for something. He roamed the tree streets. A faint light was dawning.

Luca came out of his house by chance. Aware of Norris's burglary routines, he watched while he was walking by. 'He smirked and wagged his finger, like naughty-naughty you know. I lost it.'

'I just meant to cut him. He was strong. I stabbed.'

Susan and Norris's mum held his hands on either side.

'I hurt Wilf too,' said Norris, welling up, before saying words his mother had waited decades to hear. 'I need help.'

Norris's mum nodded to Susan, who opened her sling bag and took out an object wrapped in a tea towel.

'It's the murder weapon,' said Susan.

144

WILF'S funeral service was held in the creepy Anglican chapel of the cemetery.

His mum, before she died, had bought a grave for one, not two. Felicia was surprised to find this out at the cemetery office. But the more she thought about it, the more she understood why. Hanna loved Wilf but needed time to herself.

So, his neighbours raised money to buy him a grave, because Felicia knew he wasn't a burning type. She hated the idea of him in the drum of the crematorium, where there was always another body to take his place in half an hour. She chose a burial spot near a Celtic cross, in a rough patch by a thicket, not too far from his mum.

Kevin Curran had put up a GoFundMe page on the web. It raised far more money than expected. They would build a memorial later, and he was researching sculptors for someone original. Felicia said they should sculpt him a fox.

The creepy chapel was creepy when opened in 1836. It was creepy now. Would be creepy for eternity. It was high ceilinged, slit windowed, black drapes falling seemingly for miles, a Dracula catafalque in the central aisle that, today, strived to resist creepiness with Wilf's white pine coffin lying on top.

Vince's Bros were outside forming a security shield. The media were there in force. The Bros persuaded paparazzi to leave mourners alone and stand back. In return, they swore to identify the secret location of Freddie Mercury's grave after the burial. Freddie, reasoned Felica and Vince, would approve.

Hours later, they would point to a sprawling, viciously thorny mass of blackberry brambles. 'It's in the middle,' they insisted.

Mourners arrived and seated themselves. Their faces were all familiar to Wilf. Even Pencil Ear was there, sitting beside Jim Lyon, in a suit, like a son. Mr and Mrs Gupta sat behind them. At the front, beside Felicia, sat the only stranger. Wilf's brother, Sean Leahy. Felicia found him surprisingly nice. 'Irish families go to funerals,' he explained, apologising for his presence. After a pause, he added, 'He was my brother, we don't do half-brothers, that's like half-human.'

The Vicar of St. Aubert, the Reverend Ian Lawless BTh MA, stood up alongside Wilf's coffin. Like all good priests, he knew how to do sleight of hand. As if from nowhere, he produced a copy of today's *Metro* newspaper. He tossed it onto the coffin and the congregation erupted in laughter.

When they calmed down, he said, 'Do I need to say more?'

He turned and flicked on music for the loudspeakers, filling the tall space with sound.

It was the theme tune from the British children's TV series, Worzel Gummidge. Worzel was a scarecrow.

People laughed more, then subsided in silence. When silence was perfect, the Vicar stepped forward and spoke.

'I know we all wonder why Wilf lived like he did, in the conditions he did. A falling down house. But for him, it was home. It was where his mum lived.'

'Nobody could ever really see into his mind. He had Asperger's Syndrome. So, he behaved the way he did. But he was independent. His uniqueness shone. It turned out he had a way with foxes, and none of us knew. He was ... a selective man. He selected the people he spoke to or gave news to. Us. You, we, we're his select few.'

There was a pause. The vicar started waving them up.

'Didn't he seduce us all, in a way? When he scrubbed up, he looked like James Bond.'

'Do you remember what he used to say?

'I thought, maybe instead of embarrassing ourselves by singing a hymn from a song sheet, just say it?'

The mourners now were all standing.

'On the count of three, one . . . two . . . four.'

Hrymmphh.

ACKNOWLEDGEMENTS

PROFESSOR Susan Hogan, Derby University, read the first draft and said it was too short but it kept her reading instead of sleeping. Philip Douglas, in Australia, riddled me with queries to clarify the text. Best of all, my agent, Laura Susijn, more than anyone, understood Wilf. She was here for me and here for Wilf. I can never thank her enough.

This book has been typeset by
SALT PUBLISHING LIMITED
using Neacademia, a font designed by Sergei Egorov for the
Rosetta Type Foundry in Czechia. It has been manufactured
using Holmen Book Cream 65gsm paper, and printed and
bound by Clays Limited in Bungay, Suffolk, Great Britain.

CROMER
GREAT BRITAIN
MMXXVI